The Mike Midas Publishing name and logo is a trademark of Beat Murda Music Group, Inc.

For more information on the author please visit his website: http://readmrgoodgoeshard.com or

email readmrgoodgoeshard@gmail.com

Instagram: @Mrgoodgoeshardtheauthor

Twitter: @readmggh

Printed in the United States of America

TABLE OF CONTENTS

THE CONFERENCE

BY ROBDCRUZ

"Shoes?"

"Yup."

"Camera?"

"Got it."

"Flash drive?"

"Shit. Thanks. Almost forgot about it." I rushed to the desk drawer and grabbed the flash drive with my PowerPoint on it.

My wife and I had a tradition of this checklist run-through every time I traveled for a conference. It was created out of necessity because I never had my head on straight and would invariably call from the destination whining about forgetting one important thing or another.

"How long are you going to be gone this time?" my wife asked.

"I'll be back in three days. It's just a weekend conference. No big deal," I assured her.

I was a 3rd year in a doctoral statistics program, which meant much of my time was spent sweating over some presentation, or flying to a random conference to talk to a small group of like-minded folks when we just as well could have emailed each other.

My wife, Dina, was so used to this routine she took my absence in stride. That's what four years of marriage will give you. The benign neglect of companionship. Not that I'm complaining too much. At 30 years old, Dina was every bit as beautiful as when we met when we were 24. She was 5'4", with dirty-blonde hair, tan skin, and a tight body. She worked as a personal trainer at a posh gym, so her arms were that sexy mix of slender and fit that every suburban house mom and celebrity was dying to get. And, I thank the lord every day, her fitness had spared her incredible C cup tits. The sex was still great, and she hadn't yet tired of blowing me now and then. But, 4 years married and 6 years together meant that she was allowed to be relieved to have me out of her hair for a couple of days.

I gave her a kiss goodbye, slapped her ass (as is tradition), and went downstairs to grab a cab to the airport.

Once through security, I rush to find my gate. In my head, I'm George Clooney in Up in The Air, sliding effortlessly through the airport. In reality, I'm a slightly disheveled mess, frantically searching for my gate because my flight has been boarding for ten minutes already. I finally spot it, and get on to find my seat. I plop down in a huff.

"Morning Rob. What the hell took you so long."

My friend Jessica, also in the doctoral program, hands me a coffee. We've traveled to a few conferences together and were pretty good friends, so there was an earned ease between us. This was undercut only slightly by the weird tension that often exists between opposite sex classmates. You know, the kind of the tension begs the questions- "Are we supposed to fuck at some point? We are, right? Why haven't we?" But we've never made a move. My wife has at times called her my "school wife." Not that I would mind in some ways.

Jessica was about 5'0", if that, with a healthy body, and a face that was pretty but also had "character" in the form of a bit too large nose. She also happened to have the most massive tits I've ever seen on a girl her size. Is size H a thing, cuz that's what she would have. The tits, and her extreme openness, were what made the tension for me. But like I said, nothing ever happened. I try to be a good guy and won't let anything go past flirting.

A little after take off, Jessica takes off one of my earbuds and does that loud whisper thing you have to do on a plane. "Oh man, I can't wait to get some nerdy dick at this conference. It's been a while." - Like I said. She's very open.

"You always do pretty well," I joked.

She teased back. "Hey, why don't we make sure to get rooms next to each other so you can at least give yourself some action while hearing me fuck. Or, you can finally bring that camera you are always using and take some pictures to bring back home. Is Dina into amateur porn?"

"Shhh. I'm trying to enjoy this shitty rom-com," I said, pointing at my screen. I put my earbud back in and tried to focus on Katherine Heigl's terrible acting.

With the camera comment Jessica was referring to my photography hobby. I loved to shoot people, but as I was never brave enough to have anyone model, I stuck to trying to capture candid moments. I've definitely never shot amateur porn like she was recruiting me to do. One day.....

We touched down in Houston where the conference was being held. By the time we checked into our hotel room I was exhausted. Jessica and I, by chance, did get rooms next to each other and I knew I'd be hearing her pound against the walls all night. I cycled through my memories of packing to see if I remembered noise canceling earbuds.

————

The next morning I am woken up by the sound of pounding on the adjoining room door. The pounding perfectly matches the pounding going on inside my head. Everything feels hazy.

"What the hell happened?" I say to myself. I start to tick through what I could remember in my head. The conference was the usual boring affair. I went to a few talks, and even gave a short presentation myself. I ambled around the poster presentations asking questions and appearing interested. Nothing out of the ordinary. That night, Jessica and I hit the hotel bar as we usually do, talking and getting drunk... that's all I can remember.

Boom Boom The pounding on the door continues. Purely out of a desire to make it stop and not out of any desire to actually attempt to wake up, I drag myself to the door.

I yank it open, and Jessica is standing there looking fresh-faced and rejuvenated with two coffees. "Good morning sleepyhead!" she yelled. Or whispered. I'm so hungover it all sounds the same. I recognized this version of her. This is what she was always like the morning after getting laid.

"And nice to see you again, Mr. Thickness!"

"Mr. Thickness?" I had no idea where this nickname came from until I focused on her and saw that her eyes were looking straight down at my crotch. Hanging out for the world to see was my thick cock, at about half-mast owing to the morning mood. I must have fallen asleep before I could actually get into any pajamas. I rushed to get a pillow to cover myself.

Jessica handed me a coffee as her words echoed in my head. "Nice to see you again?" Worry gripped me as I considered what might have happened. Here Jessica was, clearly having had sex the night before and she is talking to my penis like they are old friends.

"Oh god. Did we..." I managed to stammer.

"Fuck like rabbits?" she says with narrow eyes. "You mean you don't remember?"

"No. Shit! I can't believe it."

Jessica gets up and grabs my camera from the table, pops out the memory card and puts it into my laptop.

"Well you documented the whole thing. Let's refresh your memory." The TV turns on and my computer screen is visible. We always bring an Apple Tv to conferences so we can project our slides and practice our presentations on the hotel room TVs.

Jessica pulls up the images from my camera. She clicks through the first couple. Candid shots of people in the airport and the hotel. Then I stopped at one I must have taken in her room.

In the photo, Jessica is seated in her room with a glass of something strong in her hand. She looks at the camera seductively but obviously a little drunk. In the next shot, she is standing, mock-modeling for me. She's still wearing her conference skirt and blazer, but gone is the shirt underneath. The blazer is buttoned so that the lapels drape over her massive breasts, trying their best to contain them, but letting the nipple peek through slightly. Jessica clicks through a series of her posing with the blazer, stopping on one where she has her blazer off, with her bare back to the camera, as she looks over her shoulder. Her tits are so big, the sides of them can be seen even from behind.

"Jessica, I'm sorry. I was so drunk I must have blacked out. I don't remember this at all. I mean, I know we have always had this sexual tension between us, but I never meant to act on it."

Jessica was looking at me with a hurt face that suddenly cracked into a smile, then devolved into full out laughter.

"Jess? What's going on?"

Once she was done laughing and making me feel sufficiently bad, she said, "Relax Rob. We didn't exactly hook up. We got drunk and somehow got on the topic of your photography. You mentioned how you had always wanted to take pictures of people modeling rather than candids, but you never had the guts. So, being the amazing woman I am, I modeled for you.

"Oh thank god. So we didn't hook up? I don't know what I would have said to Dina."

Jessica looked a little hesitant. "Well...we didn't hook up per se. Just keep watching. You were shooting the whole time."

She clicked through the next photos and the memories started coming back.

....

I remembered taking the photos of Jessica. She was a great model as her body's curves and her distinctive face gave me a ton to work with. Plus, she basically has no shame and was open to everything. She did her best, for my sake, to cover nipples, but occasionally she would let her hand slip and I'd get an eyeful of her large areolas and hard nipples. The pictures shifted around the room. Some at the table, some at the window. The window pictures were the sexiest, but the most arousing were the shots of her on all fours, still in her skirt, with her gigantic tits drooping down.

Eventually there was a knock at the door. Jessica put her blazer back on, but left it unbuttoned so her tits were still almost fully visible. She opened the door and said "Oh finally. Get in here." Even in my drunken state I recognized the man who walked in the room. Dr. Steven Wilks was one of the most respected scholars at this conference. Everyone looked up to him because of his brilliance, but also because he was basically a celebrity level stud. Dr. Wilks was a tall black man, with a shaved head that contrasted with his trimmed but grown out dark beard. His skin was a dark brown which made his hazel eyes and bright smile pop. I've literally heard Jessica swoon during his lectures.

From the way he walked in, he appeared to be about as drunk as we were. He didn't register me until Jessica said, "You remember Rob from the bar, right? He's a big fan of your work."

"And the camera?" Dr. Wilks asked.

"Don't worry about that. I just wanted something to remember you by. Rob, you're free to take whatever photos you like." When Dr. Wilks started to protest, Jess just opened her blazer to let one of her massive tits fully fall free. He stopped talking immediately and swooped in to devour her nipple. Jessica threw her head back, enjoying his mouth on her breasts. She shot me a look and did the little "take pictures" symbol with her hand.

I shot away as Dr. Wilks stripped off her blazer and spent a while roaming over each of her gigantic breasts. Jessica unbuttoned his shirt and yanked it off, revealing a chiseled body. His dark skin was smooth, and he clearly spent as much time in the gym as he did in the library. Jessica roamed her hands over his chest and down his rippled abs. She undid his belt rapidly, like she was unwrapping a gift on Christmas she had been eager to receive.

I remember this so well, not because of the picture I got, but because this is the point that I recall becoming aware of my dick straining so hard against my pants. Watching her tits flail and her wrapped in desire was too much. When not shooting, I fondled my cock from outside my pants.

Jessica undid Dr. Wilks' pants and pulled his boxer briefs down at the same time. His cock sprung forward and out; an extremely thick 9 inches of black steel. Jessica groped and stroked it. About to get on her knees, Dr. Wilks stopped her, and took his time to pull down her skirt. He gripped her healthy ass, and explored her body with his mouth. Jessica pulled him down, and they fell together onto the bed. Their bodies were wrapped up together, as Dr. Wilks started to kiss her neck and travel down. Again he spent plenty of time, licking and sucking her breasts. He then lifted up on his knees and shoved his cock in between them. With tits like Jessica's, I imagine they are impossible to not want to fuck.

Watching his strong body thrust that cock between her tits pushed me past a barrier and I slowed down with the pictures and undid my own belt. I dropped my pants to the floor and unleashed my cock so I had easy access when I needed to stroke it. Jessica must have heard my pants hit the floor, and while her body was ravaged she looked over to smile and bite her lip at the sight of my cock. I stroked for her and wanted so badly to join in; for her to suck my cock while he fucked her tits, but I didn't dare. Somehow even in my drunken horny state, I knew there was a line I couldn't yet cross.

Dr. Wilks then shifted down, and steadying his cock with one hand while holding Jessica's knee with the other, shoved himself into her. Jessica's body arched and she moaned with pleasure. I somehow was able to capture the exact moment, showing her eyes wide with intense surprise and pleasure. His cock had to have been filling her to the brim. Dr. Wilks fucked Jessica hard, while she went to work on her clit. I watched as he pounded into her, her tits bouncing, one massive globed pushed over by her arm that descended down to rub her clit. Soon enough, her knees seemed to want to snap shut, her body shook, and she let out an intense scream of pleasure as she climaxed.

Dr. Wilks only slowed slightly while she came. When Jessica relaxed a bit, he refused to relent, and with a deft hand, flipped her over to fuck her from behind. Jessica yelped with surprise and pleasure and buried her face into the bed. The photo I got from that was of an incredible arch in her back, with her ass high in the air, and Dr. Wilks turned so you could see the full flex of his muscles as he fucked her hard. Jessica's PAWG ass rippled and waved with each pound, and she yelled with pleasure. Dr. Wilks began to moan, no doubt getting close to the edge himself.

Hearing this, Jessica moved off of him and assumed a position on her knees. She begged Dr. Wilks to cum on her face and tits, and he was happy to oblige. Jessica looked at me, and ushered me to come closer. "I want your cum as well."

I set the DSLR camera to record video and placed it on the nightstand. In a trance, watching her amazing tits, I stood side by side with Dr. Wilks and rapidly stroked my dick. I had no idea Jessica was such a cum slut. She looked up at us both, making eye contact and keeping her mouth wide open. I came hard and ropes of jizz shot across her face and into her mouth. Jessica closed her eyes, and a thick glob fell onto her eyelashes. As she moved her tongue in a circle to wipe cum from around her mouth, Dr. Wilks began to shoot his load as well.

By the end, Jessica's face was thick with cum, and her breasts were heaving from exertion and shining with semen. We stood panting and the camera shut off, presumably from running out of room. My memories were hazy after this, but I must have made it back to my room and passed out.

....

Having clicked off the video, Jessica looked over to me and said with a smile, "See, we didn't hook up. We didn't even touch."

"Are you joking?" I replied. Guilt had rushed in for breaking my sacred vow and was confusingly mixed with incredible arousal. Since I was blacked out, half remembering and half watching last night unfold made it feel like I was living it all over again.

"You need to relax, Rob. I've watched you at these conferences for a while. You're such a boring boy scout, but I can tell you have so much pent-up inside. If you were any of these other stats nerds you would have made a move on me ages ago."

"I've got a wife, Jessica. What am I supposed to tell Dina?"

"Nothing," she said, looking shocked I would even suggest something like that. You have to realize these conferences are completely set apart from the real world. Think of it like entering an alternative reality. You think Dr. Wilks is worried about what his wife thinks. Do you think I am worried about rushing home and telling my boyfriend? Half the guys I hook up with here have a family back home. Conferences are an escape. I know you've felt that too."

She wasn't wrong. These short trips away had started to feel like a completely parallel universe to the one back home. I loved my wife, but there was a little bit of a thrill - a charged energy -

with stepping out on my own in some weird city. Or of spending 99% of my trip at times in the cloistered hotel environment. You meet people, develop friendships, and rhythms become familiar extremely fast. And then once you are back home, all that is dropped completely. I felt a little calmer as I thought this over.

"Alright, I"m not jumping to tell her. God knows she won't see it this way. And I doubt she'll let us stay friends if she knew I had plastered your face with my cum."

"Mmmm, that was so hot. Thank you for that by the way."

"Shut up, jeez. I need some breakfast, and something to drink to take the edge off all this and to bring down my hangover. I'm going to shower, so I'll meet you in the lobby."

"Are you sure you don't want me to join you in the shower?" Jessica grabbed her tits and moved them around in an exaggerated way, clearly mocking me.

"Fuck you, go get ready," I shot back.

Feeling a lot better after a shower and a mimosa, Jessica and I headed to the conference. If you thought attending stats lectures was fun, try doing it while still nursing a hangover. Hoot and a half.

The highlight came when we attended a lecture given by Dr. Wilks and watched him stumble through an answer to a question that Jessica put to him during the Q and A. I laughed until I remembered that I had been in the room with them last night too. It was strange how Jess could go from my cum target to my conference buddy in just a few hours. The guilt was still palpable but there really was something about being away that made it feel separate from my real life. What happens at the conference stays at the conference, I guess.

Following the lecture, Jess and I were walking to the grand hall when suddenly someone close by said, "Great question Jess. You'd never guess you've swallowed his semen from how professional you were."

We turned around and Jess laughed and gave the girl a huge hug. As soon as I saw her, I knew I was in deep shit.

Jessica said, "Rob, remember Stacy? We all hung out for a bit after the conference in New York last year? I texted her almost all of the details about my escapade last night." Jessica had emphasized the word "almost" for my benefit, likely to signal that she hadn't told Stacy about my involvement.

"Hi. Yea I think I remember you."

This was a gross understatement. I not only remembered Stacy, I had been thinking about her on and off since we last met. I was struck so much by how beautiful she was that I would even think of her when fucking my wife sometimes.

Stacy was about 5'2", with red hair cut short into almost a pixie cut. Her skin was very fair, and brushed over by freckles on her cheeks. Her eyes were green, which sat against her fair skin and red hair so majestically. Her lips a light red that would slide easily into an adorable smile. She was like a fantasy character brought to life, glowing aura and all.

Stacy's body was slender and her limbs were long, which for some reason reminded me of a 70's starlet. This was helped by her penchant for high waisted jeans that made her ass stick out in a way that begged to be grabbed. Her tits matched her slender body, and I am betting hovered somewhere between an A and a B in size.

At that convention in NY she and I had hit it off and, with Jessica, had hung around each other for the whole weekend. If I hadn't been married I would have tried something for sure. Something told me that had I tried she would have welcomed it as well.

"Hey Rob. I caught your talk. Interesting stuff," Stacy said, with a smile.

Jessica interrupted with, "Yes, yes. All very interesting. Just one more breakout group session, and we are free for the night. Stacy, are you going to join us again? I've missed you, and I know Rob would love to bore you with the behind the scenes details of his talk."

"Yea, sounds fun," she said laughing.

After she left, Jessica and I walked to the next room for our session.

"If you don't fuck her, I'm going to scream. I didn't say anything last time, but there's obvious tension between you two."

"Jessica, calm down. Just give me some time to acclimate to this whole fantasy island thing you are onto with conferences and time away before we start talking about fucking people."

Jessica smiled a smug smile. "The fact that you didn't just break down or completely shut me up is a good sign I'm right. You want that little tittied skinny girl so bad."

I hate it when she's right.

That night we met at the hotel bar, and familiar patterns set in. We drank, talked about the day, and ate bad bar food. Jessica was off talking to Dr. Wilks and I knew where that was going. After we drank our fill, Stacy and I decided to walk around and get away from the bar noise. Everything felt so smooth as if we picked right up from the last conference. Eventually, the topic turned to hobbies and I mentioned my photography.

"I love it. I've been taking candids of people while I'm here," I said.

"So people have no idea you are taking pictures of them?" she asked.

"Yea. I know it's weird. I catch them when it's natural. I did want to get better at shooting people who are modeling, but I've been too scared to approach anyone." As I said this, images of me shooting pictures and loads of cum on Jessica flashed in my mind.

"Well, I'd love to see your work anyway."

I let the words come out of my mouth knowing full well what it might lead to. "Sure. I have my camera here. Want to have a look now?" I felt a pit in my stomach, both from the acknowledgment that I set in motion something I couldn't take back, but also from the anticipation of her answer.

Stacy looked at me, her green eyes large, and smiled. "Yea, show me."

We walked back to my room. Once inside, Stacy put her blazer on the chair. Like Jessica, she had been wearing a button up and blazer, but instead of a skirt, she wore long dress pants. On her slender body it made her look stylish. I think something else that made me gravitate towards her was that I was dying to photograph her. I knew she would look so good through my lens.

She sat on my bed and I sat next to her with my laptop. Like before, I projected the images from my laptop onto the TV. My heart skipped a beat before I remembered I had closed out the pictures that Jessica had projected up earlier. I flipped her through some of my work, all the while enjoying the fact that I was sitting on a bed with her.

"These are really good. I can't believe how intimate you can make a candid picture taken at a distance be."

"Thanks. Hold on. I think I actually have one of you from that conference in New York." I searched back to that time and found the photo.

"Oh!" Stacy was taken aback. In the photo she was seated at a table, wearing those sexy high waisted jeans and had a simple short sleeved shirt tucked in tightly. She was laughing to someone off camera, and her torso was slightly turned to make the shirt cling to her breasts, making them pop. The picture was light, joyous and with a hint of sexiness all at once.

"Shit. I'm sorry. I haven't really shown anyone their own photo before. Never really get the chance. This must seem like a huge invasion of privacy or personal space or something..." I stammered, worried I ruined the whole night.

"No. That's not it at all. The picture is great. I'm thankful you took it. I've just never seen myself like this."

"You like it?"

"I love it. You're really good." Stacy looked excited and was looking right into my eyes. I wanted to lean in, to make something happen. But she popped off the bed.

"Where can we set up?" she asked, looking around the room.

"Huh?" I was thoroughly confused.

"Set up for a photoshoot. You have your camera and you're too scared to ask anyone, so let's just go for it.

How could I say no. She was so eager, and I was definitely feeling eager in a multitude of ways.

"Umm, sure. I mean we could just take the comforter off the bed and use that as a platform."

Stacy shot me a mock scandalized look, but got busy taking the comforter off. "So how do you want me to stand?"

"Just stand up on the bed and try to act natural."

Stacy got on the bed and stood awkwardly for the first few shots. Even not knowing what to do and with shitty hotel room lights, she was incredibly stunning.

"Let me fix some lights." I adjusted the stand up lamps so her face was lit more. "Now just, I dunno, give me some laughs." She lit up the room with her smiles, and I kept shooting.

"I think I'm going to need some more booze if you want me loose."

I broke out the little drinks from the minibar and handed her one. "Uh. I'm not drinking alone. You too," she chided. We both gulped down mini-bottles of whiskey.

Stacy started to mime models she must have seen on TV. She moved her back to me, and gave me an over the shoulder look. She jumped on the bed a few times. She held her hands to her hips. I clicked away and she laughed.

"Ok, let's get serious. How about this?" she said, as she started to unbutton her shirt.

"That's good," I encouraged. Not wanting to be too eager, I added, "why don't you go slow on each button, so I can get a good one."

Stacy slowly undid each of her buttons and untucked her shirt. She let it hang there, and behind my camera I could see her silky white skin and a lacy black bra. She moved her body slowly, occasionally moving her shirt aside to reveal more skin.

"Really sexy, keep going," is all I could muster. If she were paying attention, she'd see the beginnings of my cock straining against my pants.

Stacy pulled her shirt off and tossed it to the side. Her alabaster skin on her torso, like her cheeks, were flecked with freckles. With just long pants on and only a bra, her body looked all the more elegant and sexy. I wanted to trace my finger tips over her body and hold her.

She stopped posing and looked at me. "Hey, I know how this works. It makes the model more comfortable if everyone in the room is just as naked as they are."

It was obvious what she was doing, but it worked. I put my camera down, and looking at her, pulled my shirt over my head. Stacy looked approvingly at my body. I kept in shape, so I felt confident standing there. I picked up my camera again and asked "should we keep going?"

Stacy made a few more poses, and with a little more liquid courage, started to unbutton her pants. Gone was the subtly, and she let her pants drop to the bed and kicked it to the floor. I kept taking pictures but it was getting harder to focus. She was so sexy and exactly how I had pictured so many nights in my mind. Her pale skin was glowing against her red hair. Her ass is a decent bubble against her slender frame. Although not tall, her slender body made her legs and arms seem long and graceful. Her breasts were small mounds in the lacy bra and fit her perfectly.

"Hey! No fair. You're supposed to take those pants off," Stacy reminded me. I obliged, revealing an extremely hard dick straining to get out of its constraints. Stacy's eyes widened.

I picked up my camera to keep shooting and not wanting to end our game. Stacy moved a little to model, but then laughed.

"Rob, are you going to drop the camera and come fuck me or what?"

I needed no further invitation. I placed the camera on the bedside table and joined Stacy on the bed. We connected with a kiss and I felt so much anticipation pass between us. I kissed her deeply, and she snaked her tongue around mine. We groped at each other for a while, and I finally laid down and pulled her on top of me. We kissed as she ground her panty clad pussy onto my hard cock. The silkiness of her panties rubbing me felt like heaven. She moaned with pleasure and pressed down hard on my dick.

I reached around and unhooked her bra. Stacy stood back to throw it to one side, giving me a glorious view of her tits. Perfect small mounds, with tiny hard nipples. I lifted myself up to devour each of them, giving soft nibbles occasionally.

I placed my hands on her ample ass and turned her over so she was on the bed. I kissed her body down, and lifted her ass with my hands to remove her panties. I moved my head down to her completely bald slit and began to explore her with my tongue. Stacy lifted herself up in pleasure as my tongue entered her then moved up to her clit. Her slender legs were draped over my shoulders and would press in on me as she moaned and writhed in ecstasy.

After some time, Stacy pulled me up and kissed me, getting a taste of her own juices. As we kissed she reached down and pulled my dick from my briefs. She stroked me hard. "Stand up, so I can return the favor," she purred. I stood up at the edge of the bed and removed my boxers completely as I watched her crawl on all fours to my dick. Grabbing the base, she licked the shaft and circled her tongue around my tip. The feeling of her mouth was indescribable and I wanted nothing more than to feel the warmth of her mouth envelope me. Granting my unspoken wish, she took me in and to my surprise, immediately took my entire length.

"HHHoly fuck," I groaned as she deep throated my cock. It was no effort at all for her, and she smiled each time she lifted off. She then began suck me off while making eye contact. She smiled with my dick in her mouth and got a mischievous look in her eye as she lightly dragged her teeth over my shaft. The sensation was shocking and intense and I instinctively put my hand on her head. This made her smile more, and she began sucking me off hard. Her body bent over in front of me, and her ass sticking out was an amazing thing to see. I was so turned on and could have just bust my load right there, but I had to fuck her.

When I thought I was getting too close, I pulled her off, and intuiting what I wanted, Stacy laid back. Her slender body was beginning to become flushed with red desire, and her pink slit was open for me. I grabbed my shaft and aimed it toward her, teasing her pussy with my head. Stacy moaned with delight and looked at me pleadingly. After I circled her clit a few times, I began to push myself into her. Her tightness was incredible. As I entered, she bit her lip and began to grab at her own small breasts. "Fuck me please," she begged. I pushed in hard and filled her with my whole length. She screamed in pleasure and arched her back. "Harder, harder!" she demanded. I did not disappoint and began to pound into her over and over. "Yes!" she screamed and I felt the warmth and wetness of her pussy soak us both.

As I fucked her I watched her face with her eyes closed contort in pleasure. I lifted both her slender legs up and held them with one hand, continuing to rhythmically thrust into her. I kissed and nibbled her calves, then spread her legs so each one was on one of my shoulders. The taste of her skin in my mouth was delicious and slightly salty from her sweat.

Her eyes suddenly opened in rapturous panic. "I'm close. So close. Please, Rob, will you fuck my ass?" Her eyes looked at me desperately, as if there was any way I would turn her down. "Do it now. Fuck my ass hard."

I turned her over, not giving it a second thought. She bent over, waving her delicious ass in my face, its twin pale moons split in the middle with a slightly red crease. Her pussy was soaking wet and her asshole sat puckered but ready. Stacy reached back and took some of her own wetness and dipped her finger into her asshole, then wiped more onto my cock. I had only done this once before; a wedding present from Dina.

I edged myself up to her puckered hole and slowly brought myself in. Stacy winced and moaned, but pushed back to help. I moved inch by inch into her, admiring her peach and the dimples above her ass. When I was halfway in I began thrusting in and out, pushing me even deeper with each effort. We both moaned with ecstasy. The tightness of her ass around my cock was incredible.

Once I had my rhythm, Stacy moved her hand to rub her clit. She buried her face into a pillow and worked herself hard. She then lifted her head and commanded me to fill her up as she came. I quickened my pace and the tightness of her pushed me to the edge. I tried to hold back but as soon as Stacy began screaming and moaning with the intense pleasure of orgasm, I couldn't stop.

I pushed myself deep into her and let loose my load. I had never cum like this before. It felt as if my entire being was being poured into her.

Stacy collapsed and I followed right on top of her. She panted and gave soft moans while my dick twitched and shrank inside of her. Eventually I collapsed next to her, and we kissed and stroked each other's sweaty bodies affectionately.

I felt fully present with her. Thoughts of my wife were nowhere as our relationship didn't exist in this room. Here, I could be and do whatever I desired.

Our bliss was interrupted only by the sound of my text message. When I opened my phone I was presented with an image of Jessica, a face covered in cum, smirking with a thumbs up and over each shoulder was a cock. I thought I recognized one of them as Dr. Wilks'. It was captioned, "Sounds like you had a good night! Too late to join?"

Jeez. She's crazy, I thought. But after remembering everything new that's happened, I texted back, "I'll check with Stacy..."

I can't wait for the next conference

DREAM THREESOME

BY MAMATEE

"I miss you. We should get together and catch up sometime." That was a message I received on Facebook one day. It was from one of my "girls". She had just turned 18 and I have to say I was happy to hear from her as it had been awhile. I replied to her message. "I would love to get together. In fact, if you want to, we could meet up this weekend. That is, if you don't mind D being there too." She replied that she would love to since she missed both of us and we made plans to meet up Saturday night for dinner. I immediately called D and told him what had happened and we made plans for that weekend.

Saturday arrived and we met up with her at the restaurant. She gave me a big hug and we were seated. During dinner we caught up and made small talk. Then she asked me what we were up to after dinner. "Actually we have a room down the road. Probably gonna head back there after this and have a drink or two and maybe enjoy the hot tub. It's a really nice suite. What are you up to?"

"That sounds like fun. I'm not doing anything. Probably a boring night at home with my mom and sister. Wish I could afford a stay at a hotel with a suite..."

I looked at D and he smiled. "Well you're certainly welcome to come back to the room with us and hang out for a bit if you want. We could catch up some more."

"Really? Are you sure I wouldn't be imposing on your guys's weekend?" She looked like she was scared I would change my mind.

"I'm positive honey. We would like it if you would join us."

So we finished dinner and she followed us back to our hotel room. We had a really nice suite with a king sized bed and a large walk-in shower. While she looked around the room, D brought out the root beer flavored vodka we had gotten and poured a shot. "I've never had that before. Is it good?" she asked.

"It's not bad," I replied. I can let you have a shot if you want, but that means you won't be able to leave for a while. No drinking and driving of course." I said with a smile.

"Really? Are you sure?"

"Of course hun." I replied.

So D poured her a shot and she sucked it down with a smile on her face. We all took a shot and then D lit up a blunt for me and him. While we smoked, she wandered around the room checking things out. D and I smiled at each other. We had been entertaining playing around with this girl for a long time and here we were in a hotel room with her and she was now 18 and legal. What a lucky day for us.

She came back and sat down on the bed next to me. "Can I make a confession to you?" she asked me. "Of course hun. You can tell me anything." I replied with what I hoped was a warm and confiding smile.

"I like you. Both of you."

"We like you too honey"

"No, I mean I LIKE you."

"Oh." I wasn't really surprised by this news but I tried to act like I was. " What exactly does that mean to you? " I asked her. As if I didn't know. She looked a little apprehensive, like she wasn't sure what to say.

She blushed and looked at the floor. "I have a crush on you."

"On me or on D?" I asked.

"Well both of you really. I think you are beautiful," she said to me. Then she turned to D, "and you scare me but I like it. I've always wanted to say something but I figured I wouldn't get anywhere with it because I'm so young."

D and I looked at each other and smiled. We had been waiting to hear confirmation of what we pretty much already knew. "Do you have any other confessions for us?" I asked her with a smile.

"I really like hugging you." she said to me. I like the feel of your breasts on mine. Mine are so small and I like feeling yours up against me. It's why I have always hugged you for so long." I smiled at her and urged her to continue. "I have another confession but I'm scared you will be mad at me for it"

"What is it honey?"

"There's a reason I like to park where I do. When D was still at work I liked to park next to him. I...." She trailed off and looked down.

"It's ok hun. Whatever you have to say is ok. I won't get mad."

She looked up and her face was red like she was embarrassed to tell me. "I flashed him once or twice when I was getting out of my car," she said quickly. I just smiled at her because I already knew this. D had told me when it had happened. "I knew he was in his truck and that he was looking at me. I had on a skirt and I wasn't wearing anything underneath. When I got out of the car I purposely spread my legs for him to see. I wanted to see how far I could push him. I wasn't sure if he had noticed or not because I was too embarrassed to look him in the eye after I had done it."

She looked at the floor once again. I lifted her chin and looked her in the eyes and said, "I know." She looked shocked. "D tells me everything hun. He told me right after it happened." She was looking back and forth from me to D like she couldn't believe what she was hearing. "We don't have any secrets. He tells me everything."

"I am so embarrassed."

"Don't be. We are both very flattered by your confessions. And I think we have some of our own." Now she looked confused. "I like you too. I enjoy your hugs. Look forward to them even if I'm being completely honest. As for D, well he likes you too."

She looked flabbergasted. "You like my hugs? But why? It can't be my boobs. They are so small. Especially compared to yours."

"I assure you your boobs are just fine." I said.

She didn't believe me. "But look at them," and she pulled up her shirt. "They're so tiny. I don't even have to wear a bra." My eyes were glued to her tiny little breasts. As were D's. "See? they're nothing to look at." she started to pull her shirt back down and I quickly stopped her. "Don't." I said. "You're beautiful. Your breasts are beautiful. Don't hide them." She had small, perky breasts that were maybe a B cup, but most likely were A's.

She stopped and looked at me. "Are you sure?"

"Yes I'm sure. Don't feel like you need to cover them up. If it would make you more comfortable I could take off my top too."

"Really? You would do that for me?"

I nodded and proceeded to take off my shirt too. As I did I glanced at D and saw that he was stroking himself through his shorts. She was riveted on my chest though so she didn't see it. Yet. I smiled at him and she noticed and looked over. He just smiled at her and continued to stroke himself. When she looked back my bra was gone and the girls were hanging out. "Wow!" she said. "Can I touch them?"

"Sure." She reached out, kind of shyly, and lifted each breast with her small hands. "They won't break. You can be rougher." She lifted and squeezed my breasts and rubbed my nipples with her thumbs. I moaned and that seemed to encourage her. She bent her head and sucked my nipple into her mouth. I almost came right then and there. Her mouth was so warm and she sucked my nipple just right. She moved from one to the other, expertly tonguing and sucking them. It felt so good. I opened my eyes and looked at D. He had his big black cock out and was stroking it and watching her suck my nipples. She must have sensed my distraction because she stopped and looked up at me. She followed my gaze and gasped out loud. "Wow! It's so big!" He continued to stroke it while she watched.

"Do you wanna touch it?" I asked her. She looked at me and I saw the mix of surprise and longing on her face. She wanted to but she wasn't sure I was really serious. "It's ok," I said. "You can touch it. Go on." She walked over to him and knelt down in front of the chair he was sitting in. She slowly reached out and wrapped her hand around the shaft. Her fingers didn't quite touch around his thick shaft. She slowly and softly stroked him up and down. "You can do it harder. He doesn't bite. Unless you ask him to, of course." I said with a laugh. She gripped him a little harder and smiled.

"He's so big. I can barely get my fingers around him. How do you handle this?" She kept stroking him and I could tell it was getting hard for him to handle.

"Would you like me to show you?" I asked. She sat back and released his cock. "Yes" was all she said.

D stood up and almost hit her in the face with his cock. He walked over and stood in front of me. I wrapped my fingers around the base of his cock and gripped hard just like he likes. I stroked him up and down while she watched from her place on the floor. "Come sit next to me so you can see better" I said. She got up and sat next to me on the bed. I continued to stroke him. Then I leaned over and swiped my tongue across the head. "Mmmmmm. He tastes good too. Wanna try?" I asked her, as I pointed his cock in her direction in invitation. She looked me in the eyes and silently asked me if it was ok. I nodded and she eagerly bent her head and licked the tip of his cock. Before I could encourage her more she was sliding her mouth down his shaft as far as she could. Which considering his width was not very far. She came up gagging and coughing. "How do you do that?" she asked me. "It's so big."

"I can show you," I said. She nodded so I leaned over and slid my mouth over the head of his dick and down his shaft until I could feel it in my throat. I could hear her gasping next to me in disbelief. I slowly slid back up and popped his cock out of my mouth leaving behind a trail of saliva. "Oh my god! How did you do that?"

"Practice hun. Lots of practice."

"Can I try again?" she asked. I nodded and pointed his cock at her again. She eagerly slid her mouth down his dick and quickly came up sputtering and choking again. "Guess I need more practice." she said with a laugh.

I asked D to go sit down and I turned to her and took her hands in mine. "Can I ask you some questions before this goes any further?" She nodded. "You aren't a virgin are you?" She said no so I went on. "Have you given a blow job before?" She blushed and said yes. "Ok. Do you masturbate?" This time she turned beet red and looked at the floor as she nodded. I pulled her head up by her chin and looked in her eyes. "Don't be embarrassed. You should never be embarrassed about sex. As women, we are conditioned to hide how sex makes us feel and that's wrong. You should never be embarrassed or ashamed about what makes you feel good. Do You hear me?" She nodded so I went on. "I'm asking you this so we know what we are dealing with here and whether or not this should go any further. I don't want you to feel like you are being coerced into anything. If you don't like something please let us know. We want this to be a pleasurable experience for you. Okay?" She nodded. "So tell me, what do you wanna do? Is there anything you want to know or experience?"

It took her a minute but she finally asked me to touch her. I asked her how and she said she always wanted me to touch her breasts. So I reached out and caressed her breasts and stroked her nipples with my thumbs. She leaned into my hands and moaned. Feeling encouraged I bent over and flicked my tongue across her nipple. She grabbed the back of my head and pushed me into her chest. I sucked her nipple and most of her tit into my mouth and swirled my tongue around and around, making her moan in pleasure. D got up and walked over to us. She pulled him down and asked him to touch her like I was doing. He quickly bent his head to her other tit and took it in his mouth. I thought she might come then and there, she got so loud. We continued to have her breasts for a few minutes and then pulled away. "Don't stop!" she cried.

I looked at D and then said to her," I'll make you a deal. We will do whatever you want, but you have to tell us what it is you want. No being shy or embarrassed. Just say it and we will do it." She hesitated for only a moment before she nodded and asked us to continue.

We played with her breasts for a while, sucking and biting and licking, while she moaned and clutched at our heads. Then we leaned back and asked her what else she wanted. She said she wanted to kiss me. So I leaned towards her and softly laid my lips against hers. She kissed me back eagerly and opened her mouth. It was so different from kissing a man. Her mouth was soft and warm and our tongues mingled together like they knew just what to do. I pulled away and she leaned towards D. After a glance at me, he kissed her. It was so hot watching the two of them kiss. When they stopped she reached for me again. We kissed some more while D played with her breasts. When we pulled away she dropped to the floor and took my breasts into her hands. She drew my nipple into her mouth and I moaned in pleasure at the feel of her tongue scraping across the sensitive flesh. D took my other breast in his hands and proceeded to bring me to the brink of orgasm with his attention. The two of them together almost pushed me over the edge. I looked down and watched them battle over my breasts with their mouths, seeing who could bring me the most pleasure. When I couldn't take anymore, I pushed them away and asked her, "What next?"

She was unsure so D took the lead. He stood up and pulled her up off the floor and led her to the mirror. He stood behind her while he stroked and squeezed her breasts and told her she was beautiful. I walked over and knelt down in front of her and showed her my appreciation. I sucked each nipple into my mouth and teased and tormented them while she watched in the mirror. I watched her eyes roll back in her head as I moved my way down her chest to her flat stomach, licking and kissing a path. I put my mouth over her mound through her pants. She was warm and wet,

I could tell even through her clothes. I asked her if she had ever had her pussy licked. She looked at me and said yes. I asked her if she had ever had an orgasm with another person. She blushed and said no. I stood up and we took her back to the bed. I asked her if she wanted to get undressed. She nodded so we started to undress her. First her pants came off. We laid her down on the bed with us on either side of her. I stroked her pussy through her panties while D got undressed. I got her good and wet and then slipped her panties off. D crawled between her legs and started to kiss her thighs while I finished taking off my clothes. I kissed her stomach while he moved his way up to her glistening pussy. I held her legs open and watched him kiss and lick her inner thighs. She moaned and begged him to lick her pussy. He obliged. He ran his tongue the length of her snatch, which he was very good at by the way, and it took everything I had to keep her in one place. I thought she was gonna come just from that. Poor girl, she had no idea what she was in for. He plunged his tongue into her and she came up off the bed. His tongue flicked her clit and she cried out. I rubbed myself while I watched my man lick this young girl's pussy. It was one of the hottest things I have ever seen. I went back to lavishing her tiny tits with attention while he made her writhe in pleasure.

But before she could cum he stopped and asked me to come help. I laid down between her legs and got my first good look at her young pussy. It was pink and bare and oh so wet. I rubbed my fingers up and down her slit and she was so warm. I slid my finger into her wet pussy and felt her squeeze while she cried out how good it felt. I put my face closer and smelled her sweet scent. It was time to get my first taste of pussy fresh from the source. I had never been with a woman before so it was all new to me. But I know what I like so I went for that. I flicked my tongue across her slit and up to her clit. She tasted so good. I sucked her clit into my mouth as I slid my finger in her again. All the way in. She bucked and screamed in pleasure. I felt her juices start to flood my mouth. D had primed the pump and I got the reward. As she started to cum, D shoved his cock in her mouth so she wouldn't scream out loud. She sucked on that big black cock while I made her cum with my mouth and my fingers. I was relentless and she came a couple times before I let her catch her breath.

I crawled up the bed to D and kissed him with her juices on my lips. He devoured my mouth like it was candy, the taste was so sweet. Then I bent down and popped his dick out of her mouth so I could kiss her too. I wanted her to taste herself on my lips. She hungrily kissed me till every drop of her cum was gone from my mouth. Then she asked to taste me. I said sure. I laid down on the bed and she kissed her way down my body stopping at my breasts for a few first. When she got to my pussy she just explored and looked and felt for a while. I was busy sucking D's cock so when she finally placed her tongue on me I jumped. She asked if she had hurt me and I assured her she hadn't; she had just startled me and that it felt good. That encouraged her so she went back to licking my pussy. First she just swiped her tongue up and down my slit. Then, getting bolder, she slid her tongue inside me a few times. I moaned in encouragement, and truth be told, pleasure, and she moved her way up to my clit. She sucked and licked just as I had done to her. When she slid her finger inside me I was done. I bucked and moaned around D's dick while I came all over her face. She was as relentless with me as I had been with her. I had to close my legs on her head to get her to stop.

She crawled up my body and kissed me deeply and I could taste myself on her lips. D thrust his cock in between our lips and we shared his big black dick for a while. Taking turns licking and sucking the head and shaft and kissing each other over his dick. He moaned loudly, "Fuck that's hot! Suck that dick you dirty bitches. Aw shit!" I could tell he was getting close and I was nowhere near ready for him to cum yet so I suggested we change things up. It was time for D to take a more active role in our little game. We decided to put her in the middle of us once again, but this time with me at her head and D at her pussy. He spread open her pink, swollen, pussy lips and slid his finger up and down her slit. She was so wet and hot. When his fingers were good and wet he slid one into her hole. It was so tight and slick and almost too small for his thick finger. But he managed to work it all the way in and then slid it in and out of her while she writhed on the bed. He found her G Spot and the girl damn near came off the bed screaming. "Oh my god!" she gasped. "What did you just do?"

"That, my lovely young thing, is your G Spot." D replied with a smile as he continued to manipulate her pussy. She looked like she wasn't sure if she liked it or not. But she eventually relaxed and let him make her feel good. I busied myself with paying attention to her taut nipples trying to distract her and make D's job easier. I loved playing with her tiny buds and hearing her moan. I have always had a fascination with boobs and hers were perfect. Meanwhile, D was still trying to get her to cum by rubbing that Gspot of hers. Her legs spread wider to give him better access and he pushed another finger into her pussy. She moaned again. "Oh god yes! I feel so full! I think I'm gonna cum oh god!" D picked up the pace with his fingers and bent his head to tongue her clit. That was enough to push her over the edge and she came hard. I held her down on the bed while she bucked and screamed and came all over his face and hand. "Oh fuck! Oh god! That feels so fucking good! Oh god!"

We let her catch her breath and recover for a few minutes before we moved on to the next phase of the game. D and I played with each other for awhile, kissing and stroking each other and working up to where we wanted things to progress next. I got up and went to the table in the corner of the room. She watched me and I could tell she was curious about what was gonna happen next. I opened the basket sitting on the table and her eyes got big. I had quite an array of toys and other sexual things inside. I decided to pull out my strap-on and try to gauge her reaction. She looked shocked at first and then she looked excited. She got up off the bed and came over to me. "Can I touch it?" she asked. "Of course." I replied. She reached out and touched it gently. It won't break," I said. She gripped it a little more firmly and stroked the shaft. "Wow, it's quite large. What are you gonna do with it?" I smiled and said, "What would you like me to do with it?" She seemed uncertain and was quiet for a few minutes. "Can I try it? I mean, can I try fucking you with it?" Now it was my turn to be surprised. "Sure if that's what you wanna do. I told you we would do whatever you wanted tonight." Her face lit up like it was Christmas morning. She took it from me and asked me to help her put it on. I helped her into the straps and got the dildo positioned for her so all she had to do was figure out how to use it. I sank to my knees in front of her and started kissing and licking the dildo like it was a real cock. She stared down at me wide-eyed and fascinated. But she was about to get an even bigger shock because D sank down next to me, took the dildo out of my mouth and wrapped his lips around it. Her eyes got huge as she watched his head bob up and down on the big purple dildo. He made it nice and wet and then told me to stand up and lean over the bed with my ass facing out. I did as he said. He kissed her and turned her towards me. "Look at that beautiful pussy just waiting for you to shove that big cock in it. See how it's all wet just for you? Would you like me to get it ready for you? Would you like to watch me fuck her first and make sure she's good and loose for you?" She nodded and moved off to the side, all while stroking the dildo. I gripped the bedspread and waited for him to slide his big black cock in me. The anticipation of waiting for that first entry was always the best for me. I loved feeling him slide inside me for the first time. It always felt so good and brought me close to the edge of orgasm.

So when he stepped up behind me and grabbed my waist I braced myself for that first entry. As he slid inside me, I moaned loudly, and with everything that had happened already, it wasn't long before I was cumming long and loud. My legs shook and my heart raced. I felt empty for a moment when he pulled it out, but that quickly changed when I felt him slide back inside me. Only it wasn't him. It was her and the strap-on. I felt so full. She was hesitant at first, but she quickly got over that as the headiness of what she was doing sank in. Her strokes got faster and longer and harder. I was loving every minute of it. D climbed up on the bed in front of me and I eagerly grabbed his cock and started sucking it. I loved the feel of having a dick inside me while I sucked one too. It was so hot and sexy. I had wanted to try it for a long time, and even though one wasn't real, I didn't care. It still felt amazing. I could feel myself about to cum so I bucked back against the cock in my pussy harder until my orgasm overtook me. I almost collapsed on the bed and probably would have had I not had a big black cock in my mouth choking me.

D pulled his cock out of my throat and told her to stop. That it was her turn to feel a nice stiff cock and did she want it from me or from him. I turned towards her weakly to see her reaction and she looked at me as if to ask permission. Which she actually did. "Do you mind if he fucks me first? I would really like to see what that feels like. I've never had one so big before. But I want you to fuck me too. Can you put on the strap-on so I can suck all your pussy juices off of it while he fucks me?" I had absolutely no problem with that so I nodded and got up. We figured that her being on top would be better to start out with so she could control how deep he went. So D laid down on the bed and she climbed on top of him while I put on the strap-on and then knelt on the bed near D's head. She slowly lowered herself onto his hard, throbbing cock. When she was as far as she could comfortably go she grabbed the dildo and started to lick it while she rode D's big black dick. The more she sucked my dildo, the deeper she took him into her pussy. Before long she was moaning and taking him balls deep into her tight wet pussy. "How does that feel, baby?" I asked him. "Is she nice and tight? Is her pussy good and wet for you? Does she make you wanna cum?"

He moaned and said, "Oh god yes! Just like I imagined it would be. She's so warm and wet and tight. Like a glove. I could cum in this pussy easily." I smiled and watched her bounce up and down on his dick. I have to admit it was one of the hottest things I had ever seen. Lost in her pleasure, she had forgotten all about me and was solely focused on riding that dick. So, not to be left out, I slid my pussy over his face and let him go to town. He slid his tongue up and down my slit and latched onto my clit, sucking and nibbling. I reached out and grabbed her tits and squeezed them and flicked her nipples with my thumbs. This seemed to increase her pleasure and she sat down balls deep on D's dick and cried out. "I'm cumming! Oh my god! I'm cuuuuummming!" I leaned forward and latched my mouth onto one of her nipples and sucked. Hard. She screamed and pressed my head into her chest. It was a minute or so before she could move again. I let go of her breasts and leaned back just as my own orgasm started to shudder through my body.

When I could move again, I said," My turn to fuck that pretty pink pussy". She was more than willing to cooperate and quickly slid off of D's dick. I had her lay down on the bed on her back and pulled her to the edge while D positioned himself at her head so she could suck his cock. I watched as she took him into her mouth and licked all her juices off his dick. While she was preoccupied, I slowly slid my dick into her dripping wet hole. She gasped and looked down at me sliding in and out of her pussy. She was so wet and D had spread her nicely for me. I watched as I slid my cock in and out of her cunt almost balls deep. With every stroke she became wetter and wetter. I thoroughly enjoyed watching her suck D's cock while I fucked her.

I looked down again to watch the amazing sight spread before me. Next thing I knew, D was behind me caressing my ass. He whispered in my ear, "I want to fuck you in your ass while you fuck that pretty little pussy." I closed my eyes and let his words wash over me as a shiver ran through my body. All I could do was nod because words had failed me. He kissed and bit my neck and slid his fingers in and out my pussy making them nice and wet. Then he bent down behind me and spread my ass cheeks and ran his tongue all around my puckered hole. He got me nice and wet and then slid his fingers inside as far as they could go. It was the most amazing feeling ever to be fucking her and getting my ass fucked by his fingers. I couldn't wait to feel his dick inside me too.

"Ooh you like this don't you? You can't wait for me to fuck you in this tight little ass huh? I'm gonna so enjoy fucking your ass and making you cum while you fuck her hard." I shivered in anticipation. He walked over to our basket of goodies and grabbed a bottle of lube. I tried to focus on fucking the beautiful pussy in front of me. Then he was behind me making sure I was nice and lubed and ready to take his big black dick up my ass. I bent over and kissed her while he lined his cock up with my asshole. I felt the head pushing at my entrance. I slid my dick all the way inside her and waited for him to fill me up. The head of his cock slipped in my ass with a pop and I moaned into her mouth. He gave me a few to adjust to his size and then he slid all the way in me. I came right there, screaming into her mouth. She pulled back and looked at me. "Is he fucking your pussy? Does it feel good?" She had no idea what he was doing to me. I shook my head because I couldn't speak, but that wasn't a problem because D was more than willing to tell her what he was doing to me in explicit detail. He pulled back til the head was all that was in me and encouraged me to continue to fuck her which would guide his cock in and out of me.

So we started up a rhythm. I slid back onto his dick and then slid my cock back into her and he would follow and then pull back out. We repeated this with increasing speed and pleasure for us all. Before I knew it both of us girls were cumming. I collapsed on top of her and waited for the tremors running through my body and hers to subside. D pulled his cock out of my ass with a pop and I shook all over again. When I could move, I slowly pulled my cock out of her spasming pussy. It was covered in her juices. I looked at D and told him to clean it. He dropped to his knees and proceeded to lick it clean from balls to tip. "That pussy tastes good doesn't it baby?" He nodded with a mouth full of cock. "Mmmmm I love watching you suck dick. It's so hot." I looked up and our little playmate was intently watching us. "Do you like what you're seeing, little girl?" I asked. She nodded and came closer. "Why don't you join him and show me how good you can suck a dick?" She quickly got down on the floor next to D and he gladly moved aside so she could go to work.

She licked it from tip to balls and then slid her lips over the head. I watched in fascination as she slid her lips down the shaft, engulfing almost the whole dildo. It was so hot to watch her lick her juices off my cock. Her and D took turns sucking and licking my cock and getting it nice and ready for what was to come. I asked her if she had ever done any sort of anal play and she said no. "Do you want to?" She seemed to contemplate that for a while before answering me. "I'm kind of scared to honestly. Won't it hurt?"

"At first, yes, but I assure you it feels amazing once you adjust to it. I have some smaller toys we can try first to see if you like it. Then if you do either D or I can fuck you good." She agreed to try the smaller toys and see how she liked it so I went to our basket of goodies and chose a couple of smaller dildos and the small butt plug I have. I walked back to the bed to find D had positioned her on her stomach with her ass in the air. "Mmmmmm. What a lovely sight." I said. I smacked her on the ass lightly and got a nice low moan in response. Figuring she liked it I did it again, only a little harder. I was rewarded with a loud "Mmmmmmmm!"

D got on his knees behind her and started to lick her asshole, making sure it was good and wet. She seemed to love this too if her moans were any indication. He tried to loosen her up a bit with a finger, but his fingers were so thick that it was a little much for her. So he stopped and I stepped up. I decided to start with the little Gspot toy I had. It was fairly small and I figured it wouldn't cause much pain. I lubed it up really well and slowly inserted it into her puckered little hole. "Oh God that feels good!" she moaned. That was all the encouragement I needed.

I slowly worked the dildo in and out until I felt she had fully adjusted. Her moans were getting increasingly louder so I figured she was enjoying the attention. D lubed up a slightly larger toy and handed it to me to replace the small one. I was careful and slow when I slid it in her ass, but I really didn't need to be. She was very accomodating. It went in easily and her moans got even louder.

While I loosened her ass for one or the other of our cocks, D played with her pussy some more. Before I knew it, she was cumming and begging me to put a bigger cock in her ass. I obliged and used the next size up. It was the one D and I had first gotten for our strap-on. It wasn't as big as the purple one in width or length, but it was good sized.

"I want you to beg me to fuck you in your ass," I said while I plunged the pink dildo in and out of her tight ass. D had stopped playing with her pussy and was lubing up his cock, getting ready to experience this girl's tight, teenage asshole. By this time she was begging me for a real cock. "Oh please! Please fuck me with a real cock! D please stick your big black cock in my tight little asshole! PLEASE!!!!" He was only too happy to oblige. I pulled the toy out of her ass and he positioned himself behind her. I spread her ass cheeks for him, nice and wide, so he could slide it in easier. The head went in with a pop and she cried out. "Oh FUCK!" He stopped and gave her time to adjust to his massive dick. I massaged her clit to make her more receptive to the intrusion in her asshole and when she was relaxed, he slid another inch inside of her. She moaned and encouraged him to go deeper. He slid his cock in until it was balls deep. I continued to massage her clit and within a few strokes she was cumming yet again. He smiled at me and we kissed while he fucked our teenage lover in the ass. It was one of the most erotic things I had ever participated in. I really wanted to fuck her pussy while D fucked her in the ass, but I figured another time. For I was sure this would not be the last time we played with our new toy.

I could tell D was getting close so I asked her if she wanted him to cum in her ass or if she wanted him to cum on her face. She chose to receive his load on her face so D pulled out of her ass and had her get on the floor. I held her hair back out of her face and stood behind her and watched. He stroked his magnificent cock while we both watched. It really is an amazing sight. Before long he was erupting all over her face and tits. Rope after rope of sticky cum landed on her chin and dripped onto her tiny tits. A few drops landed on her lips and I leaned over and kissed and licked her face and tits clean.

We were all exhausted and worn out. She laid on the bed for a while and then took a shower before getting dressed. She gave both D and myself a big hug and kiss. "Thank you. That was amazing. I hope we can do it again sometime."

"No thank you. We would love to play again sometime. Right D?" He nodded and gave her a swat on the ass as she turned to go. "See you later little girl" he said with a smirk

BIG FRAN

BY MRGOODGOESHARD

Impala quickly admired the house as he stepped through the door. The kitchen was spotless, as he followed her to the den. Surrounding the 80" plasma TV was comfy leather furniture, hardwood floors, and black art hanging from the walls. Her house had to be one of the nicest on the block.

"Go ahead and have a seat. Are you thirsty from your run?" she chuckled as she offered refreshments.

Angry about the wasted gizzard box, Impala decided to just go with a drink, "What do you have?"

"Shit Patron, Hennessy, I got whatever's your flavor!"

"A shot of Henny will make my ankle feel better. What's your name, by the way?"

"Francesca but everyone just calls me Big Fran. Ain't you that rap nígga Impala, that got that song '2 Guns and a Felony'?"

Big Fran recognizing him from his music put a smile on his face.

"Yeah that's me!" he said boastfully.

"I thought that was you." She cooed seductively over her shoulder as she went to the kitchen and came back with 2 glasses and the whole Henny bottle. Impala noticed her manicured fingers as she poured the shots. Big Fran walked to the window and peeked out the blinds.

"What you do nigga? The police riding full force!" she lied trying to get Impala to stick around longer.

"I ain't did nothing major, I had a little something on me so I ran the race on them." stated Impala.

"A little something like what?" Big Fran asked as she stuck her hand in her bra.

Impala finished his shot before replying, "Just a few bags of blow." He watched her produce an ounce of weed from between her breasts. Damn this bitch titties big enough to hold a few pounds, thought Impala, as he watched her untie the bag causing the room to fill with the fragrance of the high quality weed.

"Shit roll one up for us babe. You do smoke right?" Big Fran threw him the weed and a few mango Dutch Masters.

"Yeah I'll burn one with you." Impala expertly split the wrap in preparation of rolling the weed.

"Do you know "P" from QC in Atlanta?"

"Yeah I heard of him."

"You know that's my people right?" Big Fran tried to prove her story by showing him pictures on her phone.

"Okay Okay, I see you doing big thangs!" Impala brightened up as he saw the picture of Fran and "P" together.

"Damn right a bitch doing big thangs." she bragged while sitting down very close to Impala pretending to get her phone back.

"I might have to link up with you and use those star connections." said Impala, as he put the final lick on the blunt.

Suddenly she put her hand on his chest and moved her face close to his as if she expected a kiss, but whispered in his ear, "You can get whatever your fine ass wants if you play your cards right!" She slowly slid her hand down towards his crotch.

"Girl, I got too many problems to involve you right now. stated Impala, thinking he could let her down gently. He struggled to escape her grasp hoping that sparking the blunt would distract her enough to slide over.

"Hmmph, problems!? I don't do problems, I solve them." Keeping her hand on his crotch, she used her free hand to pull a knot of $100's from the underside of her bra.

Impala's eyes bulged as he saw the answer to all his problems. He knew exactly who Big Fran was now. He had heard stories of a fat chick selling weed and paying big bread for any dick she wanted. I can't fuck this big bitch, I'm too player for that shit. Nigga you a broke player, his conscience told him as he argued back and forth with himself.

Look at her chin hair and that hair on her chest! Nigga just concentrate on the good things, big lips, big titties, and that big ass bankroll. A few years ago you was fucking big bitches for free. Nigga you better drink that Henn and get it in, his conscience easily won the mental tug of war.

You right my nigga, it is what it is, Impala finally agreed with himself. He then looked into Big Fran's lustful eyes, slowly took a pull from the blunt, and passed her blunt as she slid him the Henny bottle.

After 3 big swigs Big Fran knew he would give in to her well played mission. Impala held the bottle and looked Fran in the eyes.

"This the deal girl, I owe my cousin $500, my laptop is in the pawn shop for $250, and I lost my phone. Can we trade what you obviously want for a $1000 to solve all my problems?" Impala took another deep pull from the bottle and awaited her reply.

"A businessman, huh I like that. How about I do one better. If you're willing to eat this pussy and beat this pussy. I'll give you $2000!" Fran propositioned.

Impala thought to himself. The stakes just got higher nigga, don't bitch out now. Man up to buy Diamond something nice with the change! Okay my nigga, you win again, I'm gonna handle this shit. Him and his conscience conversed.

"Money talks bullshit walks" Impala conveyed to Fran putting a huge smile on her face.

"You aint said but a word Daddy! Big Fran began pulling out and tossing the big faces from her bankroll, basically forcing Impala to down the rest of the Hennessy bottle.

Impala again found himself putting his pride to the side as the Henny numbed his feelings enough to commit to giving Big Fran $2000 worth of dick. Before he had time to change his mind she began unfastening his belt and unzipping the zipper of his jeans.

"Look, let's just be honest with each other. I know you wouldn't do this for free so just lay back and let me work my magic. You might even enjoy it!" Big Fran all but promised him as she got on her knees and gently pushed him back until his upper body leaned comfortablely against the couch cushions.

Positioning herself between Impala's legs Big Fran reached underneath his thighs, grabbed the openings of his back pockets, and slowly pulled down his jeans.

Ok! Big Fran you might know what you're doing, thought Impala, sitting there in just his jockey boxer briefs as his dick slowly awoke creating a tent in the front of his underwear.

"See Daddy, I knew if you just relaxed and let me take control, I can make your problems go away. She released his dick from its cotton prison causing her mouth to water with anticipation. Squeezing the base of his manhood created enough pressure to swell his bell head as she

tested her gag reflex by cramming as much of his dick down her throat as she could take.

"Wait wait wait!" yelled Impala as the warmth of Big Fran's velvet throat engulfed his entire shaft.

"SLUUUURPAAP!" Big Fran released just enough pressure from his meat to barely choke out, "ERGH GAH GAH ERRR SHURT TAH UCK AH!" which sounded alot like, "Sit back and shut the fuck up!" to Impala's ears.

"No! No, seriously I'm about to AHHHHHH!" was all he got out before painting Big Fran's tonsils with his spilled seed.

After wiping both sides of her mouth with the back of her hand, Big Fran kept her raising temper by saying, "Nigga I know my head game is platinum plus so don't stress about your quick ass nut, we got all night New Boo!"

All night? Nah this bitch crazy, thought Impala as he desperately formulated a plan to out smart Fran and get out of

there as soon as possible.

"Can I use your bathroom Babe?" Impala asked with the purpose of stalling until he came up with something fast.

"Sure down the hall, first door on the left. While you handle your business, I'm gonna step into my bedroom to freshen up and change into something more comfortable." Big Fran explained

from her tippy toes as she kissed him on the cheek purposely pressing her lumpy body against Impala's while lowering herself back down to the floor.

"Take your time shorty, I'll be patiently awaiting your return." was his response as she walked ahead of him adding extra emphasis to the already wobbly swish of her hips.

As soon as Impala heard the metallic click of the lock catching the striker plate of her bedroom door he quickly scanned the living room for his exit route. Still under the influence of the potent weed and large amount of Hennessy Impala struggled to think straight.

OK, nigga you got this, just concentrate, thought Impala. Nah nigga fuck that! Grab the bitch weed, phone, and another bottle out the kitchen. The coast is clear, just walk the fuck out the front door, his now drunken conscience urged him.

"Baby are you alright? Pour us another drink, I'll be out in a second. Get that dick ready for round 2!" Big Fran yelled through the bedroom door.

With no other option, Impala stole her weed, phone, a bottle of Patron, and snatched the key fob with a Lexus emblem on it that was calling his name sitting on the kitchen table.

"A drug dealer turned thief just that fast!" mumbled Impala out loud as he pocketed the keys and headed out the front door.

GRANDMA'S FARM

BY JSIPES7798

My Grandma, Hazel La Forge was a farm girl who grew up in New Madrid County, a small farming community in the southeast Missouri bootheel. The family farm was just over 2000 acres of prime fertile land bordering the banks of the Mississippi River. The property was flat and easy to plow. Each harvest was better than the previous. Great Grandpa La Forge had been offered over $1500 per acre back in the 1800s, but he wouldn't sell one acre. It had been in the La Forge family since before Missouri became a State. In fact, Great-Great Grandpa La Forge had been a Captain with the survey party of Col. George Morgan, when he established New Madrid, Missouri in 1789. He was allowed to lay claim to the farmland as payment for his service to Col. Morgan's expedition. The farm has been passed down through the family generation after generation. When a LaForge child married, that child and their spouse received two acres of land to build a home. They would continue to live on the property and share in the profits of the farm. At present, 34 families descending from Great-Great Grandpa La Forge live on the land and work on the farm.

Grandma Hazel had four siblings; all boys. She was the third child and the only female of the five children. Thomas was the oldest child followed by George, then Grandma Hazel, later Earl and Walter, the youngest boy. Her brothers were very protective of her and chased off any boyfriend that didn't meet the high standards they had set for her.

Grandma Hazel worked the farm right alongside her brothers and was considered by most as being a tough, but beautiful girl. She could toss a bale of hay just as well as any of her brothers. Her body grew strong and firm. At age seventeen she was the best liked and probably the best-looking girl in the high school. She was average height and weight. She was friendly, creative and energetic, but could also be very egotistical and a bit mean.

When she was in high school, she had sandy blond hair, a fair complexion, sparkling blue eyes, long slender legs, a firm round ass and tits that any Playboy Bunny would die for. She always wore her hair in a ponytail to keep it out of the way when she worked around farm machinery. Any other time her hair flowed down over her shoulders. Physically, Grandma Hazel is still in pretty good shape. Her tits are more substantial and probably sag because of her age. She is still an attractive woman, but now she has bronze weathered skin with some wrinkles from working in the sun, gray hair due to old age and tired blue eyes.

Shortly after Hazel's 18th birthday, she began to date a local boy by the name of Andrew Winston. Hazel's brothers gave him a tough time at first, but after they had dated for several months, her brother George started talking up a marriage between Hazel and Andrew Winston. Everyone thought George had lost his mind. Hazel and Andrew hadn't known each other long enough to contemplate marriage. However, George was insistent that they are allowed to marry and also be given a section of land to build a home. Andrew was a timid man and didn't express himself one way or the other about the proposed marriage. He just kind of went along with the flow. He was probably afraid of Grandma's brothers.

Within a month Andrew and Hazel were married, and within the following eight months she delivered a healthy baby boy. Andrew bragged about his new son, but it was rumored that Hazel's brother George was probably the child's true father. Hazel and Andrew went on to have three more children; one girl and two more boys. My Dad was one of those boys.

My name is Johnny, and I spend most of my summers working on my Grandma's farm. I call it my Grandma's farm because she is strong-willed and everyone else in the family yields to her leadership. She runs everything, and no one challenges her authority. The farm turns a huge profit every year under Grandma's leadership and the whole family delights in getting their shares. The work is, but it does wonders for my strength and weight. I have learned to handle a bale of hay just as well as any of the other farmhands.

My favorite farmhand to work with is Chester Johnson. He is a twenty-eight-year-old black man who is working summers to pay his graduate school tuition. He is working towards a Masters of Agricultural Economics. He has an undergraduate degree in business studies. He is bright and considerate, but can also be very sneaky and a bit devious.

He is an old time Christian who defines himself as sexually straight. Physically, Bob is in pretty good shape. He is tall with dark skin, black hair and dark brown eyes. Chester grew up in a middle-class black neighborhood. He was raised by his mother; his father was sent to prison when he was young and never returned. Chester is one of the hardest workers I have ever known. He has taught me many things about running a farm for profit.

Our mornings always start around five o'clock. Chester arrives at five, and Grandma serves a large country breakfast complete with eggs, bacon or sausage, biscuits or toast, and milk gravy or grits. Grandma believes everyone who works a farm should start their workday with a hearty breakfast. What one of her favorites says is; "Eat breakfast like a King, lunch like a Prince and supper like a Pauper."

We usually begin our work day cleaning the barn and pitching hay. We also have to do general handiwork like making sure all fences are intact, tend to livestock, and some plowing during planting season. I usually start in the barn while Chester helps Grandma with sorting invoices and paying bills. His college degree in business studies is why Grandma lets him help her with the paperwork.

One morning I forgot my work gloves, so I had to return to the house. I was shocked at what I found. Grandma always wears her bathrobe when she cooks breakfast. I always assumed she did that because it was comfortable. When I step through the back door into the kitchen, I observe Grandma laying on the breakfast table with her bathrobe open and no clothes under her robe.

Chester is standing between her legs. His pants are around his ankles, and his big black cock is slowly moving in and out of Grandma's pussy. They didn't hear me return to the house, so I stood frozen in place as I watched. She seems almost spellbound by his big black cock. Her legs are around his waist, and her heels are hooked around the back of his thighs pulling his cock back in every time he eases it out to the edge of her pussy. His cock looks like it is at least a foot long and she is absorbing it all in her pussy. Her pert breasts are on display, her nipples hard, her fingers running over her own body so sensually. I get hard just watching. I have the urge to jack-off, but I am afraid they will catch me. It looks like the feelings she is drawing through his hardness are just incredible. He is looking down at her lean thighs parted for him, at her graying pubic hair, and at her pussy that is instinctively squeezing and then releasing on his hard shaft.

He keeps up a steady rhythmic humping and somehow doesn't explode right away. It is a miracle he doesn't climax immediately considering the sensory overload Grandma is putting him through. I can tell by his grunting and breathing that he is close, but he apparently doesn't want it to end, so he holds on and steadily continues to pump away on Grandma's pussy. He is sweating profusely, but it looks like he never wants it to stop fucking her.

Grandma is pinching and pulling her nipples as he moves his cock in and out. She is rolling her hard nipples in her fingertips and looking into his eyes as she milks his thick black shaft with her tight pussy. I stand spellbound watching her biting her lip, and both of them moaning melodiously. He casually reaches up to touch her breasts himself, and as the rhythm between them intensifies, she pulls him down to kiss his mouth before whispering into his ear: "You feel incredible inside me, Chester. Keep fucking me until I faint again."

Her words almost make him erupt inside her, but somehow, he manages to hold on longer. But now it seems that she can't hold onto her own orgasm. Chester seems to recognize the signs of her approaching orgasm, and soon enough she is getting there. Locked together with Chester on top, the two of them seem to be trying to push themselves together, to achieve as much contact as is humanly possible. Their lips are pressed together, her breasts squashed against his chest and as he grinds his cock into her, he places his hands on her smooth butt to pull himself as far into her as possible to maximize the sensations of his cock moving inside her exquisite pussy.

Grandma is shaking and almost crying by the time she hits the peak of her climax, and if she is feeling anything like the sensations I am feeling, I can understand why. I am almost to the point of Cumming in my own pants. As she yelps and shudders, her vagina tightens around his shiny shaft, and his climax is brewing at the very base of his cock. A few moments later he lets himself go, allowing his sperm to burst forth inside her. His hot cum is bursting forth to spurt into Grandma's eager pussy. She is hyperventilating and squealing with delight.

Just as Grandma is coming down from her orgasm, she locks eyes with me. She looks stunned at first, then panicky, and possibly embarrassed. I back out the door and run as fast as I can back to the barn. Grandma apparently didn't tell Chester I had seen them. When Chester meets me later in the barn he never mentions it nor does he act as though he knows I saw them. My Grandma either didn't tell him, or he is a damn good actor.

That night at dinner Grandma doesn't say a word about the incident. She does, however, glance at my crotch several times when she thinks I am not looking. I try to fight the urge, but I get an erection that throbs uncontrollably in my pants. I start looking at Grandma in a whole different light. I had never viewed her as anything other than Grandma, but now I see her as an older woman that loves the feel of a hard cock in her pussy. I try to erase the memory of her pulling Chester's cock into her hot pussy with her heels locked behind his thighs. What's worse is that the picture keeps changing and I am seeing ME slamming MY cock into her while she screams with pleasure. I have to excuse myself from the table and go to my room where I masturbate to the most fantastic orgasm I have ever had. I shower then fall fast to sleep. I wake up several times during the night and jack off to the visions of Grandma and me doing things a Grandma and Grandson should never do.

For the next two weeks, I find myself looking lustfully at Grandma every time I think she isn't aware of my gawking. However, she always catches me. Sometimes she will smile, and other times she will wink at me. A couple of mornings she's leaned toward me in such a way I get a glimpse of her bare tits when her robe falls open. She pretends not to notice me eyeballing, but I think she is counting on me to look.

Sunday morning when everyone is at church and Grandma is in the kitchen preparing her usual Sunday buffet, I wander into the kitchen and pour a cup of coffee. I start toward the patio with my coffee, but she asks me to stay and keep her company. I took a seat at the kitchen table where I had observed her enjoying Chester's cock that morning three weeks ago. I sit quietly and admire the roundness of her firm 58-year-old butt. She is wearing black Pilates pants that hug all the curves of her firm ass. I slip away into a daydream which has me lowering those pants and sliding my hard cock between her well-defined thighs.

She abruptly shakes me out of my daydream when she says, "What do you find so fascinating about my ass, Johnny?"

"Huh…what? I'm not, uh…Grandma what are you saying," I stammer.

"Just relax, Johnny. It's no big deal. I'm used to men lusting over me", she smiled.

I don't know if I was more embarrassed for getting caught looking at her body or if I was embarrassed at the erotic thoughts I was having about her. I had no idea Grandma knew what I was thinking. I had been so careful not to stare at her tits and sexy ass while I thought these incestuous things about her.

"Grandma, I…I…I'm not looking at you like that. You are my Grandma, and that would be incest if we did anything like that", I whined.

"Johnny, I'm old enough to know when a man wants to drag me into his bed."

"No…no, you're wrong Grandma. I would never be doing anything like that to you."

"Johnny, you don't have to deny your feelings. It okay for you to have sexual desires. You are growing into a man, and a man needs the sexual relief a woman can give him."

"Grandma, it's against the law to do the things with a blood relative that I think about doing with you. It's wrong, and I shouldn't be thinking things like that about you."

"It's okay, Johnny. I have been having the same thoughts about you ever since you saw me having sex with Chester. And if you ever want to follow up on those feelings just let me know I will make myself available."

"What about Grandpa? I'm not sure he would want to share you with me."

"Don't you worry about Grandpa. He gets all the sex he can handle from me. I'm the one who can't seem to get enough sex to meet my needs. Ever since my first time in the barn with one of my brothers, I knew I couldn't live without a hard cock in my pussy every day. Look at it this way, you would be helping Grandpa out by reducing my demands on him."

"How would this work? I couldn't have sex with you while Grandpa is in the house. I would be scared to death that he would catch us and then think differently of me."

"Grandpa is going to the Regional Farmers Convention in St. Louis tomorrow, and he will be gone for the whole week. Just knock on my bedroom door any night this week, and we will talk about it and see how it goes. I won't put any pressure on you. If you decide not to do it, I will understand."

I knocked softly on Grandma's bedroom door and waited, then quietly stepped inside the room as she opened the door. Stepping inside my eyes adjusted to the half-light of the small bedside lamp. When I saw my Grandma Hazel standing by the foot of the large king bed my cock twitched. This time she was dressed entirely different from before. Gone was the bathrobe, in its place was an almost sheer soft blue teddy that accentuated her every curve. It ended right at the curve of her ass cheeks as she turned to face me. My eyes immediately dropped to the dark areolas that were clearly evident through the thin cloth.

"Jesus" I whispered as my eyes traveled over her beautiful body.

Grandma smiles when she sees that hunger flash in my eyes. "You like?" she asks.

"Oh my God" I groan, as I feel every drop of blood in my body rush to my groin, while the evidence of my lust grows stiffer in my slacks by the second.

For the last three weeks, I had been fighting off her overtures. There was something about being near her that brought out a primal need I had never experienced before, and she has made it quite clear she felt the same way.

I watched as she slightly bent at the small table, picking up a glass of Kentucky bourbon, then turned and handed it to me. My eyes had been locked to the curve of her ass through the thin nightgown. Fuck, I think to myself, she isn't even wearing panties. She wants this as much as I do, I finally realized.

"Grandma," I start to say. My voice is parched and tight as I speak. I take a drink of the bourbon, letting the liquid burn down my throat to warm my nervous belly.

"We need to talk," I say.

Grandma sighs as she takes my now half empty glass, and turns to set it on the small table again, she stares at the glass and then slowly takes a gulp of the potent liquid, grimacing as it slides down her throat.

"I know," she replies softly. "Why don't you get comfortable Johnny."

When Grandma turns back, she finds me sitting on the edge of the bed, she half grumbles as she steps in front of me. "That wasn't what I meant," she says softly. "Get comfortable" she repeats with more authority.

I knew what she meant; and while I can think of a hundred reasons not to do as she is asking; the vision of this almost nude woman standing only a foot in front of him, made all those reasons minor. Even in the half-light of her bedroom, I can see through the thin fabric of her lingerie as her hard nipples straining to be free.

My eyes drift down her body, watching her chest rise and fall with her increased breathing. My eyes can see through the thin blue material of her teddy, to her already swollen and moist pussy lips.

I undo the buttons on my shirt and slowly slide the cloth free of my chest. I see Grandma's eyes travel over my chest, hungry and needy. "Grandma," I say softly. "You know this isn't right."

"I'm aware," she tells me, as she takes my shirt and places it onto the chair. When she turns back, she locks eyes with me and steps up until her knees almost touch mine.

"Now the pants, Honey," She tells me.

"Grandma..." I try to protest.

"The pants" Grandma almost growls down at me.

Even as I raise my ass from the bed and begin to undo and slide my pants down, I try to argue even though it has gone nowhere. As the cloth slips over my hips and down my legs, my throbbing cock stands straight from my groin, silent evidence of the effect she is having on me no matter what my logical brain tries to think.

Grandma drops to her knees as her hands roughly tug the legs of my jeans free along with my boxers. Then, shuffling forward, she slips between my spread legs. Her hand reaches out and wraps around my throbbing cock.

"I know what we agreed to, Johnny," she tells me. "God such a beautiful cock" she whispers, as her hand slowly strokes up and down my length.

I could only look down and watch in stunned silence. Three weeks ago, she had been my sweet, lovable Grandma, now she has turned into a cock hungry woman who knows exactly what she wants, and plans on taking it.

" Grandma, " I try to say. "This isn't talking."

"No it's not" Grandma cuts me off. "It's sucking." Grandma's open mouth descends on my throbbing cock before I could even think to move my hands to stop her.

"Ahhhhhhhhhh" I moan, as her hot mouth envelopes me. My hips automatically come off the bed, driving more of my length into my Grandma's hungry mouth. Along with the wet slurping, I can hear her softly gag as my swollen head hits the back of her throat.

"Mmmmmmmmmmm" Grandma hums, sending a shock wave into my balls.

"Oh fuck" I groan. "Oh God Grandma yesssss"

I watch as my Grandma's head bobs up and down on me. Obscene sucking fills the room as her spit runs down my shaft. It is the most delightful sight of my life, my own Grandma sucking my cock; it makes my balls start to tighten whether I want them to or not.

"Oh, shit" I grunt. "Gonna cum, Grandma…fuck yes."

Just that quick, Grandma pulls her mouth free of my slick cock. She keeps her hand running smoothly up and down my wet shaft as she leaps to her feet in front of me.

Grandma steps closer, straddling my knees. Her breasts now only inches from my face. I can smell her perfume and the scent of her sex in the air, without even looking I knew she was wet. I tried desperately to see her face, but the hunger in my eyes made me drop my gaze, only to have my vision consumed by the swell of her rising and falling chest. I can see her nipples, like two small pebbles, straining at the blue cloth of her teddy.

"Yessssss" I groan, as I feel her grip my pulsing cock, aiming it straight up in the air.

Grandma slowly strokes me as she stares into my eyes. "Aren't you thrilled, you're finally getting to experience what you have dreamed about for weeks; or is it a bit confusing."

"Grandma" I gasp, as I feel her knees begin to flex along the outer part of my thighs. She slowly starts to lower herself closer to me, until I can feel her heat is over the engorged head of my cock.

"Oh God" I shudder as my eyes feast on her firm breasts.

I groan, feeling her lodge my hard cock between her swollen, wet lips. She hovers above my throbbing cock, perched above me. I can feel warm droplets of her excitement dripping down my shaft.

"It's simple Johnny" Grandma whispers in my ear. "Before, I just planned to tease you. I wanted to see how horny I could make you and then just let you suffer". She flexes her knees more, and with a lewd sucking sound, pulls my cock inside her hungry pussy.

"Now, I want you to fuck me." The last word came out as a small groan, as my Grandma slid down my solid shaft. "Oh fuckkkk," she hoarsely moans, feeling that wonderful fullness filling her belly.

"Oh Goddddd" I moan as I feel her vagina walls stretch to fit me. Her velvet confines are surrounding my cock like a satin glove.

"Shit" Grandma gasps. "So, fucking good." Her arms wrap around my neck as she slowly rises and falls on my lap. Her eyes glaze as she feels her belly heating up. "That's it, Johnny," she gasps. "Fuck your Grandma like the slut she is."

Grandma tightens her grip around my neck as she begins to ride my lap. She pulls my face into her heaving breasts and feels my mouth open, and sucks one aching nipple in. Wet slapping fills the room as Grandma's ass strikes my thighs every time she drives down. She can feel that sense of fullness in her belly that only her grandson could do to her.

"Suck my tits Johnny" Grandma whispers hoarsely in my ear. She shudders as my teeth gently graze her nipples.

"Fuck yessssssss" Grandma growls as she grounds her pelvis into me. "Take me, use me. Make me your slut", she urges me.

Something in me finally snaps, I reach around and grip her firm ass cheeks as I rise off the bed. Startled, Grandma wraps her legs around my waist as I stand up, her grip tightens around my neck. Her eyes grow wide as her body hangs there, suspended on my thick cock.

"Oh God...oh fuck..." Grandma moans as she feels my arms lift her body up, then slide her back down. I am impaling her on my hard cock again and again like a helpless ragdoll. She can feel the walls of her cunt tightening as she grows closer to an orgasm with every rough stroke of my cock. "You've looked at me for weeks with lust in your eyes, Johnny" her voice hot in my ear. "Now...fuck me. Make me cum like the slut I've always been."

I could feel her hot juices flowing out of her, soaking my balls and then dripping down the crack of my ass. She wants this as much as I do I realize, and I figure since we were both going to hell for it, we might as well make the ride worth the punishment. I slowly turn until I face the large bed, moving until my knees bump the edge of the bed. Like a tipping tree, I let both our bodies fall over towards the bed behind my Grandma.

Grandma's eyes grow wider as she feels us start to fall, she doesn't know what I am doing, and a quick sensation of panic ripples through her body, and then her back hits the comforter of the bed. As the bed stops her backward motion, Grandma feels the total weight of her grandson literally slams down onto her body, driving her into the mattress. Her breasts crush against my bare chest, as her nipples scrap along my skin. The motion drives my cock deeper into her than she had ever felt before, my steel hard shaft driving so deep that the swollen head of my cock jams tight into her cervix.

"Aaawwwwwwww" Grandma wails as her body erupts. It is like an instant orgasm erupts in her belly as the shock from her cervix ripples through her belly while her legs are splayed wide open, accepting her young virile grandson. Her eyes roll back as a white explosion erupts in her head. "Johnnydddyyyyyyyyyyyyy" she screams as her entire body convulses in pleasure.

I raise up on my arms, looking down at her. I can see her body convulsing under me as I feel her hot cream gush out to soak my cock, then puddle on the bed under her ass. The sweat glistened on her forehead as her face turned into a replication of primitive craving. Her eyes only show white as they roll back, and I can feel her nails drag down my sides like claws.

"You wanted me to fuck you" I grunt. My hips pull back, only to slam down hard into her again and again. I watch her breasts shake as her body bounces on the mattress.

I feel like some possessed animal as my hips rise and fall, trying to drive my cock even deeper into her. I can hear my balls smacking against her slick body with every forceful thrust. I realize, with a sick sense of perversion, I need this, want this. We have gone past not only having sex, but even simple fucking has been cast to the wayside. We are rutting on the bed like a stag and a doe in the woods.

"Yesssssssssss" Grandma screams as her cervix is repeatedly struck by my thick cock again and again. "God fuck me harder Johnny" she moans under me. "Take me...use me" she babbles as her body races toward another orgasm.

I can feel her heels drum against the bed as I pound my body down, watching her tits shake every time I slammed into her. Grandma is grunting and cursing with every stroke as I ravage her. I watch as a small trickle of her own spit runs from the corner of her mouth and down her chin. If she wants her grandson to fuck her, then I am going to fuck her like never before.

Grandma can feel me picking up speed as I hammer into her wet pussy. She is stuttering and stammering and can't even form words to describe what is happening to her body as her own grandson takes her to sexual places she had never experienced. Her nails again rake down my side as she tries to pull me even deeper into her wet hole. She is digging into the soft flesh of my ass cheeks until she almost draws blood; all her mind knows right now is she wants more of me inside her.

"Ohh fuuuuuuuuuck" Grandma screams, as another orgasm roars through her like a flash fire in the forest. "Don't stop, Oh God, please don't stop" she begs. She can feel each orgasm rolling together into one continuous wave of raw pleasure.

"Stop?" I growl above her. "I've just started baby," as my hips pound down into her bouncing body.

Grandma tries to cry out again, but only a whimper comes from her lips as I own every inch of her. This is the reason she invited me to her bedroom this evening. She wanted and needed to be fucked like a wild animal. I can feel her belly tighten and then flex with each wave as I assault her body; my pelvis is grinding down into her pulsing clit.

"Can't...take...more" she gasps with each of my thrusts. "Please...cum."

"You want your grandson's hot seed," I ask. I can feel my balls tightening as my cock begins to swell inside her.

"Please, I want...unnnnnngggggghhhhhhh" Grandma rapidly devolves into whimpers and grunts as I drive myself so deep inside her, she can feel the head of my cock pressing through the opening of her cervix. As her eyes roll back again, her mind numbly wonders how I can be so deep as to fuck her very womb.

While another orgasm comes tearing through her shattered body, she gives herself to me, her young horny grandson.

"Joo...nnyyy...fuck...meeee" Grandma grunts out between hammering strokes. "Fill...me...with your cum...pleeeasseee."

"Oh fuck, Grandma!" I roar above her, as I feel my nuts tighten and then explode. Right or wrong, I know no one made me cum like this. My whole body vibrates as I can actually feel my hot cream as it speeds down my shaft and erupts from the tip of my cock and buries inside Grandma.

Grandma feels her mind almost blank as my sperm washes her pussy walls then shoots deep into her belly. "Yes...yes...yes." she chants as her body erupts again. Her lust hazed mind , not even able to count the orgasms as they blended together. Not even in her wilder days of high school had a man made her body respond this way. It is like an addiction, a craving she has to fulfill to survive. The fact it is her own grandson driving her to these heights, only makes it hotter for her.

"Mmmmmmmmmmmmm" Grandma coos, as her body feels that afterglow spreading through it. "Oh my, God...Johnny can you fuck" she whispers.

"Grandma" I pant into her ear. "This is so wrong, and we both know it."

Grandma's eyes drift open, and she stares up into my face. She can see the look of guilt that is written there, and yet watch the lust still burning behind my eyes. She knows it is time we did 'talk.'

"Roll over," she tells me, as her arms wrap around my sweaty back.

As ordered I roll my body over, until I lay on my back on the rumpled bed sheets. Grandma can't stifle the soft grunt as she settles onto my still hard cock buried inside her. It stretches far up into her belly, and as she looks down at our joined bodies, she says, "Jesus you're deep inside me."

I gave a half smile as I looked up at my sexy Grandma. My hands are resting lightly on her firm smooth thighs, "You're fucking tight Grandma."

Grandma rocks her body, starting a slow and deliberate motion. She can feel my cock slide about halfway out of her pussy before she lets her body drift back down on me. My thickness is scraping her walls with my veins as pleasure ripples through her.

"Your girlfriend's tight too isn't she" Grandma grunts as she drives down onto me.

"Oh God, Grandma," I groan. "Don't..."

Grandma bends forward until her face is close to mine, eyes locked. The sound of her ass slowly smacking against my smooth thighs fills the room.

"How many times Johnny?" she asks softly. She sees the look in my face. "That's right; tell me, how many times you have fucked your girlfriend in the last three weeks."

"Grandma...I can't" I try to grunt out between strokes.

Grandma tightened her muscles making the walls of her cunt grip me even tighter and then slowly dragged her tightness up my full length. She feels me shudder under her as her vise-like cunt grips my cock. She knows I can feel every inch sliding out of her as she rises up.

"Tell me" she growls; then slams her soaking pussy down onto my raging hard cock.

"Oh shit, maybe twice" I grunt under her. This time she is the aggressor, and what she is doing to my body is driving me insane.

"Twice" Grandma smirks above me. "I've fucked your Grandpa and Chester's brains out ten times each in the last three weeks." She grunts. "More than they've had in the last three months; and, they both say it's the hottest sex they have ever had."

I'm stunned at Grandma's admission. My hands reach around and grip her firm ass cheeks, as my hips thrust up to meet her downward motion.

"Your Grandpa was lucky to make it every two weeks before," she admits softly. "He says I am having my second puberty and he loves it."

"See Johnny" Grandma groans as she feels my full length drive up into her. "We can't stop. For one, we NEED this, and we both fucking know it. Second, it's the best damn thing to happen to BOTH of us."

"Do you think about me, when you're buried inside your girlfriend?"

"Oh God Grandma," I gasped. My cock throbbed deep inside her.

"It's OK Johnny" she whispers. "From now on, every time I cum on Grandpa's cock, I will be thinking of cumming on this fucking monster of yours!" I can feel her juices gushing out, knowing they are making a slick puddle under her ass on the bed.

"Oh my God Grandma, oh sweet Jesus" I lay my head back as my eyes start to roll upward.

"That's it Johnny" Grandma hisses in my ear. "Cum in your Grandma again, fill my cunt with your seed."

"Cummminnnnnggggggggg" I roar as my second load of the afternoon jets out to flood Grandma's drenched pussy. First one, and then a second-thick rope pumps up into her willing body as she rides me. She now has total control of my body as I feel myself emptying my balls up into her clenching heat.

"Oh shit yes" Grandma gasps. "I can FEEL you cumming in me."

I can't even answer as my body thrashes under hers, forcing Grandma to dig her nails into my back just to hold on. Grandma threw her head back and hung her mouth open as her belly gave a lurch, while the hottest words I had ever heard poured out of her.

"Oh fuck, I'm going to cum" Grandma wails. "Cumming on my Johnny's coooooooocccckkkk."

I can only watch in wonder as my Grandma convulses on top of me, her nails digging into my back, as her pussy walls spasms around my cock. I can feel her hot juices literally squirt out of her to cover my balls and drip down my sides as she floods me with her own desire.

Exhausted and sated, Grandma collapses down onto my body, as my arms wrap around her trembling body. I'm not sure how much truth there is in what she said, but I did know; I couldn't give this up any more than I could give up breathing.

Grandma lay gasping on top of me. Only knowing that she is damned if she is going to give up the hottest sex, she has ever had in her life. Grandson or not, the only thing she cares about is the cock slowly softening inside her, and the hot come leaking out of her satisfied pussy.

As I held my Grandma close, I wondered where things were going. The sound of her labored breathing fills my ears. As we both catch our breath, I ask, "How can we continue to do this after Grandpa comes back from the convention?"

"You leave that to me. If I can work a fuck in every morning with Chester, I can sure find a way to fuck my Grandson every day."

Tasha's webcam show Ch

2 by Daddydick89

Tasha continues her webcam show, with an unexpected surprise from her new lover Bullet.

It's been two weeks since my last live webcam show, where I ended up getting fucked by my dog Bullet and sucking my little brother C.J's cock live on webcam.

With everything happening so fast, I didn't realize how much my life had changed after that night.

I was no longer known for shaking my ass and masturbating for my webcam fans, I was now the black girl who not only likes doggy cock, but I also engaged in incest with my younger brother.

I felt a bit humiliated in the beginning, for doing such nasty things while a bunch of strangers watched online. But once I realized how much I enjoyed fucking my dog and sucking my brother's cock, I began to relax. Not to mention all of the money my freaky show generated that night.

Who knew that black bestiality and incest would be such a turn-on for so many people? But after raking in $5600.00 that night, I knew that I had found my nitch!

I lied to my brother, telling him I only made $1500.00 that night. So his cut was only $750.00. But he no longer cared about the money. He was more interested in getting his young cock sucked again.

"Come on Ta-Ta, suck me off again," says C.J. as he strokes his big cock over his shorts.

"Who says I ever intended on sucking your big cock again? It sure as hell wasn't me!" I shot back. Knowing that I fantasized about sucking his cock again. But he doesn't need to know that.

I could tell that C.J. was up to something when he walked into my bedroom and locked the door. I looked over at him as he hopped onto my bed with me.

"What do you want, C.J.?"

I say as I shoot him an evil look.

"First of all, lose the fucking attitude. Secondly, you still need me to keep your little secret, don't you? Plus, today is my birthday. So come on sis. Hook a brotha up!"

"FUCK" I shout out loud, for forgetting that this little punk was blackmailing me.

"Okay, calm down you little shit! We can work out an agreement. Yes, I need for you to keep your big mouth shut, and no I don't want mom and dad to find out about me and Bullet. But I'm sure you wouldn't want me to tell them that you made me suck your cock either."

"No, I don't"

"Good. Now that we've got that out of the way, let us get down to business."

I began to pace back and forth, trying to come up with a hot idea for tonight's show. It wasn't long before I came up with the perfect theme for my freaky fans.

I hopped back onto my bed next to C.J, to tell him what I had planned.

"Since today is your birthday, I'm going to make you my guest of honor for tonight's show."

"Fuck, yeah"

"I thought you might like that."

After informing my brother C.J. about my plans for tonight's show, I took Bullet to the backyard and gave him a good bath. Making sure to scrub his big doggy cock really well.

I wasn't sure of what I was going to do with Bullet during tonight's show, but the thought of sucking Bullet's big doggy cock was making my pussy wetter than ever before.

So that night after my parent's left, I went out to the backyard to smoke a blunt with C.J., then I started to get dressed. Since tonight's show was going to be special, I decided to wear something extra sexy for my fans.

Instead of wearing my normal t-shirt and booty-shorts, I wore my black leather mini skirt, with the matching leather v-neck top that really showed off my amazing tits.

After turning on my music and setting up my camera, I heard C.J. entering my bedroom. "Okay birthday boy, have a seat" As I pointed to the chair I had placed in front of the camera.

I was searching through my phone for my playlist, when I felt my dog Bullet brushing up against my leg, eagerly waiting to bury his big doggy cock into my hot pussy again.

"Calm down boy, you'll get your chance," I say as I pat him on his furry head.

It was showtime! So with the music blasting (When We - by Tank) and my brother C.J. sitting down in a chair, patiently waiting for his birthday surprise. I slowly make my way in front of the camera and begin to give my brother C.J. his first ever lapdance.

I was so high and so turned on, that my pussy juices were already flowing.

As I gyrated my hips and ass on C.J's raging boner, I could feel my little brothers breathe on my neck, making me even hotter. So, when he began to kiss the back of my neck while squeezing my tits through my top, I couldn't help but let out a moan.

"Oooohhhhh, Goddammit C.J!"

I say, as I bite my lower lip and begin to play with my hot snatch.

I was so turned on that I didn't realize that C.J. had now picked me up and thrown me onto the bed.

"I'm about to suck on your juicy clit Ta-Ta!"

Say's C.J. as he slowly removed my skirt and my top, leaving me totally naked, and at his mercy.

I watched as my little brother C.J. undressed, letting his thick 9-inch black dick rest on his leg, with lots of precum oozing from the tip. As much as I wanted to suck my little brother's cock again, I wasn't about to pass up the chance of getting my pussy eaten. So, I just laid back and let it happen.

I could tell he was no amateur pussy eater because he knew exactly what he was doing. Unlike most young boys his age, who can barely find your clit. C.J. took his time.

First, he took his time and kissed all around my pussy, before gently blowing on my throbbing clit, then sticking out his tongue and licking me from my asshole, to the top of my clit, all in one motion.

"Oh shit C.J. don't stop! Eat my pussy you sexy motherfucker!"

As C.J. continued to suck on my clit while shoving two fingers into my pussy. I began to pound my fists into the bed, as a multitude of orgasms ripped through my body.

"Oh my God, C.J. please don't stop!"

After sucking on my pussy and bringing me to multiple screaming orgasms, C.J. finally took off his t-shirt, showing off his chiseled chest and 6-pack abs.

As he climbs on top of me and starts kissing me while stroking his big cock.

"Do you want this big cock Ta-Ta?"

He says while looking me in the eyes.

"Maybe"

I shoot back. Trying to let my little brother know that I'm still in charge.

"Don't act like you didn't enjoy sucking my dick the other day"

He says with a cocky smirk upon his face, as he slides two fingers into my dripping snatch. Bringing me close to having another orgasm.

"Oh shit, give me that dick baby"

I say as I slide down underneath my brother's hanging cock.

With my brother still fingering my twat, I began licking the underside of his cock, all the way down to his huge swinging balls.

"Oh, goddamn! I knew you wanted that dick! Put that dick in your mouth, Ta-Ta!"

And I did. Before licking the tip one last time, then taking all 9-inches down my throat.

I felt like such a nasty bitch, knowing that thousands of strangers were watching my little brother turn me out.

But that was only the beginning. Because what happened next, was about to take things to a whole other level.

With my brother sliding his cock in and out of my mouth, while he was squeezing my tits, my dog Bullet decided it was time for him to get involved.

Soon I felt Bullet's rough tongue lapping at my clit, causing me to take even more of C.J's cock down my throat.

I was in pure heaven with my dog happily licking my cunt, while getting T-bagged by my brother.

I know my fans had to be enjoying tonight's show. Because I was getting even more turned on, knowing that we were being watched by total strangers.

After Bullet had licked me to multiple orgasn's, C.J. thought that it would be a good idea if he and Bullet switched places.

I was kind of nervous at first. But the more I thought about sucking Bullet's big doggy cock, the hornier I got. Soon, I was eager to suck my dog's cock. I patted the bed a few times, as Bullet hopped up onto the bed, with his big cock already out of its sheath and swinging between his legs.

It didn't take long for Bullet to figure out what was going on. Because before I knew it, he had made his way over to me and lifted his furry paws up on the headboard above me, before inserting his slimy doggy cock into my throat.

Within a few seconds, my dog Bullet was rapidly face-fucking me with his cock. Letting the head of his long slimy doggy dick hit the back of my throat, while his fury tail wagged across my sensitive nipples, causing me to shiver and quiver in ecstasy.

As I began to gag on Bullet's cock, I could feel my brother C.J. lifting my butt off the bed, then placing a pillow underneath me, before rubbing lube onto my asshole, then inserting my favorite 12-inch black dildo into my puckered asshole, while gently rubbing my clit.

I'm an anal lover, so I began to bounce my ass up and down with each stroke, trying to take more of my dildo into my ass, as I continued to suck my dog's cock.

Then, without any warning, Bullet's cock suddenly erupted. Sending Bullet's doggy cum straight down my throat. He must've saved that load for a while. Because no matter how much I sucked and swallowed, he just continued to skeet hot doggy jizz down my hatch.

To my surprise, Bullet's cock was still hard when he finally pulled it from my mouth and sat down next to the bed.

Meanwhile, C.J. was slowly removing my huge dildo from my asshole, which made a loud pop sound as he pulled it out.

We both stared in amazement at the puddle of my pussy juices that had managed to soak the middle of my mattress.

I was just starting to catch my breath when C.J. hopped on top of me and started kissing me passionately. I figured he wouldn't kiss me, knowing that Bullet was just unloading a shit load of cum in my mouth. But he continued to kiss, bite, and suck all over my lips, before flipping me over and lowering my dripping snatch onto his rock hard cock.

His 9-inch cock wasn't quite as big as Bullet's massive 10-inch doggy cock, but it still took me a few strokes to get acclimated to his size.

He went back to kissing as I bounced my ass up and down on his huge cock. Soon I was cumming and cumming hard.

"Holy shit C.J. you're gonna make me cum! I'm gonna fucking CUM!"

As I was cumming on my brother's cock, I felt C.J. tap the bed twice, making Bullet hop onto the bed, and before I knew it Bullet once again had his paws on my back trying to mount me. Only this time he entered my ass.

And in one long, deep stroke all 10-inches of Bullet's doggy cock went straight up my ass. Causing me to break my kiss with my brother and grip his shoulders hard and scream

"Oh my God, you sick motherfucker! You made him fuck my ass! This is soooo fucking nasty! Soooo fucking nasty, C.J."

But C.J. just smiled and plowed my pussy, while my dog Bullet was balls deep in my ass.

With Bullet's doggy cock deep in my ass, my brother C.J's cock began to press against my g-spot, making me squirt all over him with each stroke.

"Fuck...fuck...FUCK I'm cumming!!!!"

I could feel C.J. reaching up and spreading my ass cheeks, allowing for Bullet's big cock to go even deeper into my bowels.

"Holy shit, Ta-Ta. I can feel it! I can feel Bullet's cock rubbing against mine! I'm gonna cum! I'm gonna fucking cum! Aaaagggghhhh!!!!

Debauchery

And as my brother pumped his load into my cunt, I felt the knot at the base of Bullet's cock making its way into my gaping asshole.

"Oh no, that's too much! He's too fucking big! Make him stop C.J.! Make him stop!

Then I felt Bullet's cock explode deep inside my bowels.

As Bullet's doggy cum was spraying my insides, I noticed that C.J. had a frightened look on his face. I figured that some of Bullet's cum must've dripped on him. But once I heard my father's voice say.

"What the hell is going on in here?"

I knew we were in for a long night.

To be continued....

86

My White Boy Sissy by Wolf Hunt

Daniel Martin…

That kid is picked on more than most people in this school. Mostly because he's small, meek, and looks more like a girl than most of the girls in this school. I wouldn't say he's skinny because he's got the widest hips I've ever seen, but his upper body is the stereotypical nerd torso.

His ass though… Damn, he's got an ass most girls would be jealous of. Most of the time I can't stop thinking of what it would feel like to have my big black dick 9 inches deep in that ass. Or his pink luscious lips wrapped around it.

Unfortunately, being the starting wide receiver for Santa Barbara, I've got a certain rep to uphold. And it wouldn't look good if I was seen banging a band sissy. Especially a geek like Daniel who's the target of many bullies. Everyone takes a shot at that kid.

But still… it's very tempting. What I would do to get him under me, taking my dick like a good little faggot.

Sitting in math class is a rather bore. Fortunately, Daniel's in my class. Today he's wearing those skin-tight jeans and an Aratheon t-shirt that clings to his skin.

The worst or best part of school is I'm stuck with this eye candy all day long. He's in every single one of my classes. The kid's smart, there's no doubt about that. Don't get me wrong, I'm not the typical stupid ass jock. My parents made sure of it. My dad is a successful entrepreneur. He demands excellence from me, both on the field and in the classroom.

As we pile out of class after the bell rings, I trail that sissy to our next class. A few people give me high fives and tell me what a great game I had last Friday. Some of my teammates hit me up, but I keep my eyes on that fat ass of his.

"Move it, fucking faggot," Brett Marshall says as he wacks Daniels books out of his hands, scattering all over the hall. Brett's a punk, but he's my teammate. Great linebacker and starting power forward on the basketball team. We're not friends by any means, just teammates.

"You don't have to be an ass, Brett," I say as I kneel down to help the guy out. He looks up at me with those sky blue eyes. I can see he's on the verge of crying and all I can think about is how hot it'd be to shove my dick down his throat.

I just want to grab his messy brown hair and fuck his face.

"Why are you being nice to me?" he asks.

"Not all jocks are assholes," I tell him as I hand him his books. "Why do you haul all these books around?"

"My locker is on the other side of the school," he says, brushing his hair out of his face and adjusting his glasses.

"That sucks," I say, while I get a good glimpse of that ass as he bends over and grabs the last of his books. I just want to yank his pants down, spread them cheeks and drill that ass until I deposit a big load of semen in it. "By the way, I noticed we're in the same math class."

"We're in all the same classes," he says as we continue on to our Gov class.

"Right... You know, I could use a study buddy like you," I admit. Not that I need someone to help me with math. Math comes easily to me. I just want an excuse to get him over to my house... Alone.

"Like me? You mean, you want someone who'll do your homework for you?" he asks.

"Do I look like I need someone to do my homework? I'm not the stupid jock you might think I am," I tell him. "I just want someone who takes their class work as seriously as I do."

His face turns bright red as he tears his eyes away from mine. "I'm sorry... I didn't mean to assume."

"It's all good, I'm just messin with ya. So what do ya say? Study buddy?" I ask. His eyes go wide as he looks back up at me.

"Uh... sure! Okay, yeah!"

"Great! Why don't you come over to my house after practice and we'll finish up the math homework and study for the upcoming test," I suggest.

"Yeah... except, I don't have a car..." he says.

"No problem... If you want, you can wait up here and I'll give you a ride after practice," I told him. "Hell, you can even watch us practice if you want."

"Really!?" he asks. "What about Brett?"

"Don't worry about Brett," I tell him. "I'll make sure no one picks on you."

"Really?" He looks up at me with those eyes... Eyes as blue as the ocean. His face just has that natural innocence about it. It makes my dick hard.

"Yeah... stick with me and no one will touch you." Nobody but me.

As we make our way out to the practice field I see Daniel off in the corner with his books. I can't believe he came. He's a gazelle in the lion's den. He looks up at us as we start stretching. "Oh my god, wow... What's that faggot sitting on our field for?" Brett asks.

"Hey, leave him alone, he's my little faggot," I tell Brett.

"What!? Did you jump to the other side?" he asks.

"What if I did? I mean, you can't tell me you wouldn't want that sissy's lips wrapped around your cock? I bet he's got the tightest asshole ever."

"Wow, you are a fag!"

"If getting your dick sucked is gay then I'm a total fag."

"He's kinda got a point," Adam says. "Ain't nothing gay about getting your dick sucked. Besides, nerdboy over there looks more like a girl than half the sluts you've slept with, Brett."

"Whatever…"

Coach blows the whistle and we get practice started.

After doing some sprints and drills, we ran some plays. Out of the 8 passes that were thrown to me, I didn't drop a single one.

When practice finally ended, I was quick to tear my pads off and leave. I find Daniel waiting for me outside. Fuck, if he grew hair out a little longer, I wouldn't be able to tell if he was a guy. Especially with that ass. Perfect bubble butt. And his lips, definitely dick sucking lips. I'm going to be having this sissy sucking my big black cock by the end of the night...

Gear in one hand, I sling my other arm around his shoulder. "Let's head over to my house."

Leading him over to my convertible Audi, I toss my shit in the back and hop in the driver's seat. He meagerly climbs in and we're off.

It doesn't take long before we roll up at my house. His eyes light up as we pull in the drive. I don't think he's ever seen a house this big. "This is where you live?" he asks.

"Yeah, where did you think I lived, some fucking ghetto? Just because I'm black doesn't mean I'm poor."

He tenses up.

"Relax, I'm just fucking with ya."

We get out and head in. I put my hand on the small of his back and led him through the large glass door.

I toss my shit down and lead him up the giant white staircase to my room. Once in my bedroom, I gestured to him to sit down on the bed and start tearing off my clothes. "I'm going to take a quick shower and wash the stink off if that's alright with you."

As soon as I pull my trunks down, his eyes go straight to my flaccid 8-inch cock. "Uhh... Yeah... sure."

"You act like you've never seen a dick before."

Immediately his face burns bright red as he looks up at me. "I... I..."

"Want to touch it?"

His eyes go wide. "What!?"

"Do you want to touch it," I make sure to emphasize every word.

"I... uh... I'm not gay."

"I highly doubt that. Come on, no straight boy would stare at a cock like that."

The way he bites down on his bottom lip makes my dick twitch. I don't know how much more of this I can take. I just want to dominate this little sissy white boy and make him my bitch.

I start stroking my cock as I slowly walk up to him. My dick is literally only a couple of inches from his feminine face. He can't take those baby blue eyes off it. Slowly, I run my fingers through his soft brown hair, grabbing a handful and pulling him closer to my cock.

His luscious lips touch the tip of my dick. His reluctance shatters as he parts his them, letting the head of my cock slip in.

His eyes look into mine as I pull his head down on my cock, shoving more of it into his mouth. He gags as my dick reaches the entrance to his throat. Both of my hands have fists full of his hair and I start feeding him my cock, using his mouth as a pocket pussy.

His dainty little hands run up my thighs my cock pushes against his throat once more. Tears well down his eyes as he spits and coughs on my dick. He tried to push off, but I held him there. "Swallow it, baby."

Those baby blue eyes close shut. My dick plunges down his throat as he opens up, swallowing it whole. His nose bumps into my pubes as I hilt my dick balls deep inside his mouth. I can see his neck bulge out as my dick clogs his throat. He's going to make one sexy ass sissy when I'm done with him.

I let go of him and my dick pops off his mouth as he coughs and gags. "Take your clothes off."

He looks up at me all wide-eyed like a doe in the headlights. "Wait... what?"

"You heard me, I want you to take your clothes off."

"But..."

"No buts, I want to see that beautiful body of yours." I pull him off the bed and take my seat on it, all the while stroking my big fat dick. "Don't be shy, let me see all of you."

He stands there lost for words. I guess I'm going to have to give him a hand. The poor kid's probably frozen with fear. So many kids body shame the poor boy for having such a girlish figure, he's probably ashamed of it.

I pull him closer as my fingers find the bottom of his shirt. I slowly pull it up and over his head. His skin is pretty flawless. Not chubby, but not too skinny either. He's got a flat stomach and chest. My fingers rub up against his nipple and slowly make their way down his stomach, such soft skin. I unsnap his pants and slowly drag them down. No way! He's got on Aratheon underwear. They hug his fat ass perfectly. Almost like panties.

This white boy was made to be fucked.

He holds onto my shoulders as I lift one leg after the other and drag his pants off. I see the tiny bulge in his underwear, rubbing my hands over it, his little pecker is as hard as a rock. I give him the turn around sign with my fingers and he hesitantly shows that ass to me.

Sinking my fingers beneath the hem of his underwear, inch by inch, I pull them down revealing the sexiest ass I've ever seen. Not a single hair below his head.

I give his ass a hard slap, making him groan out. He looks back at me. "Why are you doing this?"

I pull him down in my lap. "Because I want to make you my bitch. Here's the deal, Daniel… You become my little sissy slut and no one… not even Brett will ever bully you."

"Wha… What's that entail?"

"Obviously that means not only are you going to be my personal cock sucker, but I'm going to fuck that tight ass of yours whenever I want."

His eyes go wide. "I don't know… Won't that hurt?"

"For the first time, yeah, it'll hurt. But I promise, once that ass gets stretched out, you're gonna love it. You'll crave for a big black dick."

My hand slides down his back causing him to tense up. I grab his ass as my fingers zip down the crack of his butt finding his tight little rosebud.

"How badly do you want to be popular?" I ask him. "I can make that happen. As long as you submit this ass of yours to me and become my bitch."

Before he can even say anything, I grab his hair and pull him in for a kiss. My tongue batters its way into his mouth as my finger sinks into his tight asshole. He squirms as my digit sinks to the first knuckle.

"Now, if you want my protection from Bret, get on your knees and start sucking my dick."

He bites his lower lip as he looks into my eyes with those baby blue orbs. As the last bit of his resistance diminishes, he sinks to his knees and slips my cock between his lips. "That's it, bitch. Suck my big black dick."

I grab a handful of hair and start bobbing his head up and down on my cock. "Urrghh, fuck… Wrap those dick sucking lips tightly around my cock and suck."

His cheeks collapse as he inhales my dick like a popsicle. "That's it, now swirl the tongue around the tip of it."

He obeys, giving the head of my cock a girl swirly. "You're a natural cock sucker, you know that?"

Those eyes as blue as the sky look up at me as his cheeks turn a rosy shade of pink. "Don't be embarrassed, it's a compliment."

I slam his head all the way down, popping my dick inside his throat. His nose once again meets my pubes. He coughs and starts choking on my dick. I pull his head up off my dick. As my cock falls from his lips, he coughs and gags up spit. With my other hand, I grab my cock and start smacking those beautiful lips. Then I plunge my cock back between his lips.

With one swift move, I flip him on his back, resting his head on the bed as I stand over him, sinking my cock down his throat. I start fucking his face hard. My balls slap his chin as my cock slams down his throat. Tears fall from his eyes as I continue to hump his face. The sound of him gurgling and choking on my dick fills the room.

I slide my hand through his hair and grip a handful as I use his mouth as a fuckhole. He just takes it. To be honest, degrading him like a whore isn't what I truly want, but I can't help myself. Whenever I'm around this beautiful girly boy, I lose control. Primal instincts take over and all I can think about is breeding him like a bitch.

As long as I'm being truthful to myself, I actually like him. Not just as a fuckhole or because he stirs some deeply filled lust within me, but I honestly have a crush on him. I actually like all the geeky things he's into. I'll never admit it to my teammates or parents, but deep down I'm kind of a nerd too.

And while I'm being honest, as I sink my dick down his throat. I want to make him my girlfriend. Yes, I mean it. I think he'd look amazing in a dress with some makeup on. Some soft lace panties, maybe one of them training bras. I'd take him on dates. We'd see one of those Aratheon movies. Then we'd spend all night with my dick up that tight ass of his. I'd fill his thicc bum up with load after load of my seed.

Speaking of cum, I'm about to blow a load down his throat. "Fuck!"

A riptide of pleasure crashes through me as my cock explodes down his throat, shooting a thick load of cum straight into his stomach. He coughs and sputters as I pull my dick out, leaving the tip still inside his mouth. I drop another load, filling up his mouth, a little bit of cum drools out between his lips. Like a good little sissy, he swallows it all. And you know I've got to mark my territory.

So I pull my dick from his lips and paint his face with one last load of cum. Damn, he looks so hot with my seed all over his girly face.

"Now it's official, you're mine."

He goes to wipe his face off. "Unless you're going to swallow all that cum, leave it."

He looks up at me with those eyes as blue as the ocean. The look on his face is one of fear, shame, and humiliation. Part of me wants to pull him into my arms and kiss him. Tell him everything's going to be alright. The rest of me wants to fuck him like a slut and continue to degrade him.

I take my finger and swipe up a load of cum just below his eye and feed it to him. He licks it up without hesitation.

"I'm going to take a shower, feel free to lick the rest of it up."

It doesn't take long to clean myself up. I walk back in my room to find him fully clothed and the cum off his face is mostly gone. I shed my towel and his eyes fell down to my cock. "Don't worry, baby. You'll get more of this dick. Tomorrow I'm going to pop your anal cherry and make you fully my bitch."

"Please... Please don't tell anyone about this."

"Ha... who gives a shit what other people think. I want the entire school to know you're mine." Wrapping my arm around his waist, I pull him close to me and press my lips against his. I stroke his cheek with my thumb as I wrap my hand around his delicate face. He melts in my arms as my tongue explores the inside of his mouth. My other hand sinks down and grabs his ass.

Finally, I let go of him and broke away.

He bites his lip as he looks up at me with those sapphires. "Aren't you afraid people will find out you're gay?"

"Is it really gay getting your dick sucked? Or fucking a hot little sissy like you in the ass? I don't think so. Besides, who's going to say something to my face? And to be honest, I don't give a shit if it's gay or not." I grab his hand and lock my fingers between his. "Now come on, I'll take you home."

"But... If people find out that I sucked your dick, they're going to humiliate me," he says as I lead him downstairs.

"Trust me... By tomorrow, everyone's going to know you sucked my dick. No one's going to lay a finger on you or say a word."

"What!? But... How?"

I stop as we reach the bottom of the stairs and lift his chin up to me. "I'm going to make damn sure everyone knows you're mine. If anyone even says a word to you, I'll kick their ass. Didn't I tell you I'd protect you?"

He nods his head. "Now let's get you home. Tomorrow's your first day as my girlfriend."

"Girlfriend? What!?" His eyes go wide.

"Didn't I say I was going to make you my sissy bitch?" The look on his face is priceless. "Don't worry, we'll take it slow, but eventually, I want you to start wearing panties, a dress, and some makeup."

"No, I can't do that! What am I going to tell my foster family?"

"Why not tell them the truth? You're really a sissy deep down and now you're finally embracing it."

"Please, don't make me do it."

"Hush, baby. Don't worry. As I said, we'll take it slow."

As we walk out the door, Tanesha, my fraternal twin sister pulls up in her Camaro. "Oh my god! No, you didn't! Did you finally fuck that white boy!?"

"Relax, he just gave me a blow job. I'm going to pop his anal cherry tomorrow."

She laughs her ass off. "I can't believe you're actually going through with it. Let me guess, you'll want me to get him all dolled up next?"

"Tanesha, you know me all too well… It's like we're twins or something."

"Shit, I'm going to have so much fun with this white boy. By the time I'm done with him, he'll look hotter than most of the bitches in our school. I've always wanted a gay friend like him to go shopping with and dress up."

"Alright, well I gotta take him home. I'll talk to you later."

It doesn't take us long before we're at his house. Kinda run down shabby ass shack, really. I sink my hand in his soft hair and pull him in for one last kiss before he quickly gets out. I can't take my eyes off that ass of his as he hustles inside, giving me one last glance before disappearing behind his front door.

I can't wait for tomorrow!

THINGS GET WILD IN AFRICA

BY BRAVEBOMBADIER

Back in the fifties and sixties, my father worked in Tanganyika or Tanzania as it's now called. I was then twenty, I was in the British army, based in the UK and I had saved up two months leave having been given permission to take an extended leave to visit my parents.

They lived at the time in a very remote area with only a small handful of European engineers and a number of Indians, mostly Sikhs who occupied mainly admin roles.

I quickly realized how boring those two months were going to be, with nothing to do after the initial bit of exploring the local bush. Which was quite dangerous due to the abundance of wildlife, snakes, spiders, etc. So I didn't do too much of that.

I had been there a few days and was wandering around looking for a suitable piece of wood to make a catapult.

"Hello," said a quiet voice behind me. I turned around and there was this pretty little girl, maybe eighteen years old. "Are you Mr Grant's son? Oh sorry, silly question really because you must be".

"Yes, I am," I said, "My name's Peter or rather Pete, who are you?"

"I'm Jane, my dad works for your dad at the depot. I've seen you knocking about and you really do look quite fed up already and I hear you've got a couple of months here".

"You're not wrong there," I said, "I really don't know what to do with myself".

"Have you seen the bats yet?" Jane asked.

When I shook my head, she said "Come on then, I'll show you. They're in the mango trees over by the hill". So off we went, a few hundred yards and there were dozens of mango trees.

"You can't eat the mangos," Jane said, "They're the wrong type but they do make good chutney. Follow me to that big tree over there but look out for snakes, there's lots of them around here".

The tree was big, like a huge umbrella and very dark up in the canopy. One huge branch had deformed and was growing out from the tree parallel to the ground and three or four feet above the ground.

"If you sit up there and look up and after a bit, you'll be able to see all the bats hanging near the top," she said. I climbed up a bit awkwardly but eventually got myself perched on the branch and looked up. Quite quickly I found I could see hundreds of bats, clustered all over the place.

"I can see them," I exclaimed looking back at Jane.

She wasn't looking upwards though, she was instead looking at my shorts. I suddenly realized that with all the maneuvering when getting up, my cock had come out of my underpants and she must be able to see it up the inside leg of my shorts. She hadn't noticed that I had looked down at her and her gaze was transfixed on my cock. She's probably never seen one before I thought. Feeling a bit embarrassed, I turned sideways away from her and looked back up in the tree again.

When I looked back, she had also moved around, so she could see my shorts once more. My cock had, of course, developed a mind of its own and had begun to grow. You dirty sod I thought. But for some reason, I just turned my head to look up at the bats again.

When I took a sneak peek down, I saw my cock was actually just sticking out from my shorts down the side of my leg. Jane just stared, her eyes wide and mouth hanging open in amazement.

Enough of this I thought, time to stop. But I realized that there was no easy way of getting down without exposing yet more cock. Oh well, best to just be as quick as I can.

As I tangled my body to drop down, Jane suddenly said "Here let me help, it's quite high" and just as I started to drop she reached out with both hands to steady me.

One hand was fine, catching my arm. But the other somehow ended up going between my legs with the palm of her hand firmly pressed to my cock. She jumped back with a girly squeal as if bitten and we both turned quite red in the face.

Completely lost for words, we just looked at each other for a moment or two, until I said: "Come on, let's go back and get a cold drink." And so we wandered back in silence, not sure what to say.

A few days later, as I went out the back, I saw Jane hanging about obviously waiting for me to appear but too shy to call for me.

"Hi" I called, "You okay?"

"Yes I'm great," she said with a cheery grin, "My sister Mary has just arrived back from boarding school, she'll be along soon and you can meet her." Almost as she finished speaking, this beautiful girl came round the corner.

Wow, I thought. She's stunning, totally gorgeous. She wore a small pair of shorts that accentuated her superb shape and didn't leave very much to the imagination. Her tight top showed the lovely swell of her boobs.

After introductions, Jane said, "Mary wants to see the bats, are you coming?"

It was a bit odd, I thought, that she must have seen them before. Then with a flash of inspiration, I thought I bet it's not the bats she wants to see, I think Jane's been telling tales. "Hold on a minute, I'll be right back."

I nipped indoors to my bedroom, dropped my shorts and removed my underpants and then replaced my shorts. I thought, perhaps this holiday isn't going to be so boring after all.

So off we went, chatting away, I found both girls were very easy to talk to.

We arrived back at the mango tree and without being given any choice in the matter, Mary said, "Here we'll help you up" and almost grabbing hold of me I was bundled up onto the branch.

Knowing what the girls expected, my cock didn't wait for me to think about it but immediately started rapidly growing in size. Making sure that my legs were spread enough to allow a view up my shorts, I looked up in the tree.

I had pulled my shorts down a bit lower as I didn't feel right about my cock sticking right out and anyway it would be interesting to see how hard they looked for it.

Out of the corner of my eye, I saw Jane give Mary a nudge and she moved over a bit to make room for her to get the right view. I saw Mary put a hand to her face which had a look of glee on it.

No wonder I thought, as I could feel my cock growing bigger than ever and even though my shorts were lower, I could tell it was showing out again by the burn of the African sun on it.

I moved myself about a bit while pretending to be looking for the bats but kept an eye on the girls. Jane was smiling broadly as if to say "I told you so." Mary was obviously fascinated.

I could tell she was getting aroused as I could clearly see her nipples standing out, which I hadn't been able to see before. Enough for now I thought and suddenly dropped down which in doing so, gave them both a real good eyefull.

We wandered about for a while until Mary asked Jane "Have you taken Pete to see the lake yet?" When Jane said she hadn't, Mary suggested we might go there this afternoon if I wanted. "It's quite lovely there, I think you'll like it."

So having agreed to meet them at two, we went home for lunch.

Two o'clock soon came and with a bag of drinks, I went out to meet the two girls. To my surprise though, there were now three. The new one being a very pretty young Indian girl and about the same age as Mary. She was dressed in very colorful traditional Indian clothes, so there was no way of knowing what her figure was like.

Mary said this is Mandi and explained her real name was very hard to pronounce in English so we call her Mandi.

Mary had two long stout sticks and passed me one. "To keep the snakes away," she explained.

And off we set along a rough, hardly used path. I went last, very happy to walk behind Mary and watch the mesmerizing sway of her hips and those clear to see bum cheeks.

I saw her glance round several times and I was sure she just wanted to see if I was checking her out.

It was quite a way and took us about half an hour to where the pathway turned round some acacia trees and then I could see the lake, it was indeed stunning. Surrounded by trees on three sides and the other rising up to a small hill with huge boulders protruding at the top.

"We always sit up there," said Mary "There's a better view and less wildlife on the big flat rock over there. It's not really safe down by the water, there are supposed to be lots of very poisonous water snakes."

We climbed up and Mary took a blanket from the bag she was carrying and spread it on the ground. I took out the drinks and passed them round. It had been hot work getting there. I was sitting at the highest point, it was quite a large flat area with the rock sloping gently towards the lake. The girls sat in front of me looking towards the lake.

Mary lay back with her head towards me, then she rolled over onto her tummy and passed the drink back up. I could see that her eyes had gone straight between my legs. I was sitting with my knees drawn up resting my chin on them. Her eyes had done their magic and I could already feel my cock stirring.

As I gazed about the lake, I could clearly see her give Jane and Mandi a little nudge. Both girls also rolled onto their tummies and I could see all three resting their heads on their arms but all looking up at my shorts.

Whilst I busied myself having a drink and looking about, I could twist my body from side to side, knowing my cock was coming more and more into view and by now was rock hard. Mandi's eyes were huge with surprise, she'd probably had a strict and sheltered upbringing. The other two girls, who had already seen it before, just looked enraptured. I could swear there was a gleam in Mary's eyes.

I just continued to sit admiring the view, pretending to be completely unaware of anything else.

I suddenly noticed that Mary had slipped an arm under her body and I could just make out her bum was moving about a bit, so I knew she was rubbing herself between her legs.

I could see that I wasn't the only one to notice, as Mandi was glancing at Mary with a shocked look on her face. Jane didn't appear to realize what was going on, I thought.

I lay back, which was a mistake as my cock then wanted to stand upright but although it strained against the edge of my shorts, it couldn't go any further. But I could feel it had started to twitch with the effort, which they must all be able to see.

Mary stood up and came to lie beside calling for Mandi to lie on my other side. Jane meanwhile, just kept staring.

Inching herself closer to me, Mary whispered, "We didn't see any snakes on the way here today but we've seen one now!" She giggled and continued, "I didn't know whether to believe Jane when she told me about what she had seen the other day but I do now. None of us have seen one like that before although we talk about them a lot at my boarding school. Mandi's a bit shocked but I can tell that she's fascinated, so don't worry."

I then felt her hand lightly stroke the outside of my leg, until after a little while she asked "Do you think that I could touch it, it won't bite will it?" and again that lovely giggle.

"No it won't bite but it might spit a bit, so go ahead."

"Jane doesn't go to boarding school, she's been schooled at home so doubt she's talked about ......er," she paused, "cocks before but I know the dirty little girl has been pinching some of mum and dad's naughty books, so she's read about it but never seen anything till you showed up."

With that, I felt her hand move slowly up the side of my leg and then pushed my shorts up a bit. Naturally, upon being freed from its restriction, my cock jumped up into full view, standing smartly to attention.

Mary's hand moved straight to it and her fingers gently caressed it, exploring her first touch of a cock. She let her fingers slowly tease all over and then said, "Come on Mandi" Mary said, "have a feel, it's beautiful."

Mandi reached over very tentatively but Mary grabbed her hand and pulled it to me. She wrapped Mandi's fingers around my cock with hers on top of Mandi's and then started to slowly move them up and down.

"This is what the girls at school say you do, is it right?" asked Mary.

"Yes, it's right but you do know what will happen if you keep doing that"? I asked.

"I think so but it's only what I've heard" Mary replied with another of her giggles and they continued with their rubbing.

"I think I should maybe take my shorts off Mary, or they're going to get a bit messy."

"Wow! Really! That's a great idea," she said enthusiastically.

So the next thing, having taken my shirt off as well, there I am lying completely naked and two young girls working their hands up and down.

Mandi suddenly said, "It's gone all slippery just like you've oiled it."

"That's my pre-cum, it's coming out of the end if you look and oil it is exactly what it's meant to do." Both girls moved in for a better look as I could feel more oozing out.

Then I felt a light finger touch the very tip and glancing down, I saw that Jane had moved up, not wanting to be left out of the fun, she was now lending a hand also. She just ran her fingers round and round the end, spreading my pre-cum.

What a great day, I thought. Three lovely young girls rubbed my cock for me.

I let my hands move and touch the side of Mary and Mandi's thighs and gently caressed my fingers.

Mary who was now lying on her side immediately bent her left knee up and she took my hand in hers and moved it between her legs. I gently rubbed the front of her crotch through her shorts but when I tried, I couldn't get under the edge of her short legs, they were much too tight for that.

I felt her fiddling about and she again took my hand and moved it to the top of her shorts, I knew that she had just undone them for me. "I've never been touched by a boy before and only once a little fiddle by a girl at school."

I moved my hand down inside and realized that just like me, she had come out with no panties on. My fingers quickly found her slit which was already very wet and slippery.

At the same time, I had moved my other hand up Mandi's thigh until my fingers were at the junction between her legs. But unlike Mary, her legs remained tightly closed so I just slowly rubbed one finger up and down her mound where I knew her clit must be, although I couldn't feel it through her clothes.

Meanwhile, at my other hand, my fingers had indeed found Mary's clit and I was giving it a good playing with. I could feel her body writhing against me.

She kissed my cheek and whispered in my ear "Please put a finger in me, I want to feel you touch me inside." So of course, I obliged and slowly slipped a finger inside the juicy warmth of her. She thrust against my hand as I slowly worked the finger in and out. Then I eased another in and I wanked her with my two fingers. She was now gasping and kissing at my neck

I felt one hand leave my cock and suddenly Mary had grabbed Mandi's head and pulled her into the other side of mine. I could see her resist at first but then she seemed to give in and lay her head against my right neck.

I turned to face her and before she could pull away, I planted my lips on hers. For a moment she seemed as if turned to stone but then I could feel her slowly relax and she let me kiss her. After a little while, I teased my tongue gently between her lips and again I could feel her reserve but I persisted and suddenly her mouth opened to me and my tongue found hers as we kissed, slowly becoming more and more passionate.

My right hand suddenly found it now had space and I knew she had decided to open her legs to me. I eased my hand down and gently caressed her through her clothing. I could feel her getting more excited so I moved my hand to the top of her trousers. I gently stroked her belly then very slowly eased my hand down inside her trousers. Although I felt her tense, she didn't stop me.

And then I had two pussies to rub.

I realized that I was reaching my own climax. "If you watch girls now, you will see what happens."

Whilst I continued to administer the two writhing girls I arched my back as I could feel the heat rising in my now very swollen cock, still being vigorously rubbed by three hands.

Four faces gazed at my cock, three in anticipation, as it started to throb wildly, until woosh and the first load of cum shot into the air. The girls all squealed with delight and amazement while my cock carried on shooting more as they wanked at it. Soon it stopped and I lay back exhausted.

Mary said, "Hey you've stopped doing your job, do you mind!"

Mary and Mandi both lay back and I felt their legs open wide so I could more easily continue. I felt Mary easing her shorts down her hips, giving me better access to her inner warmth.

Then I knew that Mandi was going to climax as I felt her stiffen and raise her hips off the rock. She suddenly gave a yelp and started to buck up and down against my hand, her head twisting from side to side. I could feel the wetness on my hand as she clamped her legs tight around it, trapping my fingers inside her as she spasmed over and over.

Mary said, "My god Mandi, that was beautiful to watch, I hope you're gonna do the same for me now Pete."

It was then that I realized that whilst bringing Mandi to a head, I had stopped working on Mary. I said, "Let me just give Mandi a kiss and then I'll be back to you".

Mandi put her arms around me and squeezed hard as I lent in to kiss her. When we finished kissing she said to me "That's never happened to me before when I've played with myself. It was wonderful. I'm sorry I tried to stop you but I was afraid and anyway, I didn't know it would be like that".

We kissed again until I eased away and turned to Mary. "Ok, now it's your turn to be beautiful." Her shorts were still only halfway down, so I eased them off of her, then went round to kneel between her legs.

"Hey what are you doing?" she asked.

"Just wait, you'll love it," I replied.

Spreading her legs a little wider so I could better see the wonderful sight of her little mound topped with the finest small blonde hairs, her slit looking very wet and inviting. I eased the lips apart as I bent closer to see her clit, not big but protruding quite proudly. As I leaned in and gently tickled it with my tongue she gasped and pushed hard up against my mouth. Ouch! I thought I'll have a sore lip later.

I slowly licked my tongue downwards along the length of her pussy. Her hands came up and grabbed a handful of my hair, pulling me into her. She raised her legs and wrapped them around my back as I sucked and licked.

I pushed her legs up higher and was rewarded with the sight of her beautiful little arse hole. Naturally, I allowed my tongue to move down till it found the small orifice which I gently tickled.

"Oh my god" I heard her gasp out through clenched teeth as I continued to work on her arse hole.

I tried pushing my tongue further in but she was too tight so I went back up to work on her clit. At the same time, I eased two fingers into her cunt, getting them nice and juicy, then moved one back down to push gently against the opening of her arse.

I had moved my thumb between her lips and as she raised her hips to meet my tongue and thumb, my finger eased its way into her arse. I could feel it clutching as it fought to resist this new invasion but then relax as my finger slipped right in. I was now finger fucking both her cunt and arse.

It was then that I noticed both Mandi and Jane were leaning over to get the best view of what was going on. Jane had a hand between her legs giving herself a little rub.

Mary released her grip on my hair and took hold of the two girls hands and pushing up her top, she placed their hands on her gorgeous tits, furiously rubbing their hands over her nipples. Both girls looked quite shocked but didn't pull away and quite soon both were busy caressing Mary's boobs, as I continued to thrust my thumb in and out of her pussy, whilst my finger kept up it's reaming of her arse hole and my mouth sucked on her clit which was by now quite a bit bigger.

I knew she was near as she writhed and bucked her pussy against my mouth. Then her hips rose right up and with a huge shudder, she started to quiver as she reached her climax. She was gasping out loud as suddenly my face was soaked with a mixture of pee and come. I thought if I don't suffocate, I'm gonna drown here as she continued to squirt.

The writhing subsided and she lay back gasping. She opened her eyes, looking at me shocked. "I'm so sorry, I feel dreadful. I just peed in your face."

I moved up and gently kissed her, "Don't feel bad, in fact, it was lovely and you tasted beautiful. I loved every moment of it."

"But I peed!" she said.

"I know and I hope you do it every time we do this."

"Really?" she asked.

"Yes, really," I said.

"And you pushed a finger up my backside! I've never done that to myself, it was lovely but I was a bit shocked at first."

She then just kissed me again and afterwards she asked: "Is that me I can taste?"

"Yes it's great isn't it," I answered.

We both then glanced at the other two girls. Mandi looked ecstatic but Jane had quite a frown on her face although she was still rubbing herself.

"What's up, little sis?" Mary asked her.

Debauchery

Hesitantly Jane said "Well it's alright for you a lot but what about me, I'm not having much fun! Well, I am really, it was fun watching but I want my turn."

I looked at Mary who just grinned and gave me a little nod. So I said to Jane "Would you like to slip your shorts and top off?"

"I thought you'd never ask," Jane replied and without further hesitation, her clothes had gone, panties as well.

She lay down between us and we feasted our eyes on the petite young body. Her breasts were smaller than Mary's but with much larger areolas and with stiff upright nipples. There was the merest whisper of hair over the top of her tight little slit.

I asked Mary and Mandi to play with her pert nipples as I bent to gently rub my fingers over her pussy lips. She quivered, her eyes closed as I eased her lips apart. And what a lovely sight it was. A tiny little clit, just sticking up but her pussy was already wet, her body had reacted and aroused itself watching her sister being brought to a climax and the little rub she had been giving herself.

I licked my tongue up along her slit until I reached her clit then closed my lips around it and gently sucked. She gasped and almost at once I felt it grow just a bit. I eased a finger into her pussy but not too far. But she pushed up hard against it. I could feel the resistance it came up against and I didn't want to break that, so I quickly eased out a bit and then back in a little again, as I gently wanked her.

Like her sister before, she raised her legs around my upper back. I tickled her arse hole but didn't try pushing my finger in, although I then lowered my mouth until I could flick my tongue around the tight little hole. She squealed with delight and pushed her arse against my mouth. I moved my hand back up to her clit but found another hand there already.

It was Mary who was busy rubbing and pulling at her clit. So I slipped my fingers back in her pussy. Whilst Mandi, I noticed was now sucking Jane's nipples which I could see had grown quite remarkably.

Her young climax came with almost no warning. She convulsed and shrieked out loud as it hit her. The joy and passion evident on her face as she rode the wave.

Then my head was soaked as just like her sister, she started to pee. Each time she arched her back another squirt of pee hit me in the face, which I had raised to watch. I could see Jane watching me wide-eyed as I opened my mouth and took all she could give.

Soon it stopped and as she lay back she said in a begging voice, "Do you think you could kiss me like you did Mary and Mandi?" It was a tentative kiss that she gave and I knew that she had never been kissed before. So I let my lips gently caress hers until I slowly eased my tongue into her mouth. Our tongues met and danced around each other as she hugged me tightly. Soon it was a lovely kiss.

When we, at last, broke for air, she said "Thank you so much, that was wonderful, the kiss, and the er whatever you call it. The best day of my life yet. And I saw you drinking my pee, wow!"

We all had a hug and then lay back for a rest and a drink.

Meanwhile, I had forgotten about myself but I suddenly noticed my cock had raised its head again, not a surprise really! Three girls all giggled and made a grab for it, as one.

Mandi whispered in my ear, "It's against everything I've been taught" she said, "But I think I'll have to let you take my trousers down tomorrow and let you do what you did to Mary. If you want to, that is?"

She gave me a beautiful smile when I said: "It would be my greatest pleasure Mandi." And you know what? I knew it would be. So here's to tomorrow.

It wasn't too long before my cock decided to let loose, the three girls all trying to catch more cum than the other. Mary, obviously the more forward of the three, then raised her hand to her mouth, stuck out her tongue and gave her fingers a lick. "Mm, that's nice," she said, "come on girls, try it." Which of course they both did.

Then Mary asked, "Jane and I both peed when we came, I don't know about Mandi but you didn't why's that?"

"Well I can't pee when I'm rock hard, I have to wait until it's nearly soft," I answered.

"I think you should show us tomorrow then, don't you agree girls?"

Looks like tomorrow's gonna be a good day!

After dressing, we gathered up bits and pieces and climbed back down from the rocks and we set off back along the path.

I slipped one hand down the back of Mary's shorts and she was soon wiggling her arse on my finger. My other arm was round Mandi's shoulder and I had reached down for a handful of lovely soft tit.

As for Jane, well she just glared and poked her tongue at me, then said: "Don't worry, I'll get my own back later." She seems to be growing up fast I thought.

After dinner, I had gone outside for a smoke when I noticed there was someone over at our mango tree. Sure enough, when I got there, Jane sat up on my branch. She had changed and was now wearing a skirt and top. "It's my turn," she said and opened her legs to reveal a bare pussy staring at me. "You like the view?" she asked, grinning like mad. "You don't need to just stare you know, you can touch, I liked your tongue playing with me the best."

So obligingly I leaned in and ran my tongue along her pussy lips. I licked and sucked as she wriggled about until she suddenly said: "I'm going to fall, catch me quickly!"

I made a frantic half grab for her but she came off the branch too quick for me to get a hold of her and I felt myself falling backwards. I landed on my back with a wallop. Jane followed me down for her to land on top of me, still straddling my face.

She didn't pause to ask if I was okay but just pushed her pussy down on my face and started to rock back and forth. "I want your finger up my arse like you did to Mary please, I want to know what it feels like," she said.

So I squeezed my hand under her so as to lubricate my finger and moved it back to her tiny arse hole. Gently I pressed but it was so tight not much seemed to happen until she suddenly pushed back hard against my finger and it started to go in. "Ouch," she exclaimed but didn't stop pushing until my finger was well and truly buried up her backside.

She rotated her hips so her pussy smashed down hard on my mouth and her arse swiveled about on my finger. "I'm going to do it, I can feel it happening again," she exclaimed as she tensed above me, her hands pulling on my head and then started to buck up and down, "I'm sorry, I'm going to pee again, I can't help it."

Of course, I couldn't answer with her thighs clamped around my head and her pussy jammed into my face.

And then a stream of hot pee was filling my mouth and although I swallowed as fast as I could, I still felt I was going to choke. I think maybe she realized and eased herself up, although maybe it was just that she wanted to watch. But still, she kept on squirting every last drop onto my face, while she watched with a rapt look on her face.

Slowly she stood up, looking a bit unsteady on her legs but with a huge smile on her face. When we calmed down a bit, she suddenly said: "I want to see you pee now".

So I eased my shorts up and took out my cock.

"Can I hold it while you do it?" she asked.

But I answered, "No, best not to because it'll go hard as soon as you touch it and I might not be able to pee then."

"Oh okay, then will you pee just a little first so I can see what happens?" With that, she knelt down to watch closely as I pointed it away from her and started to pee with a satisfying woosh. "Stop!" she commanded, "now point it at my mouth and start again."

Not thinking about her clothes, I did just that and began peeing straight in her face, she opened her mouth wide and just drank it down, her mouth coming closer and closer to my cock. As I stopped she leaned forwards and put her tongue on the end and licked at the drips.

Of course, my cock reacted immediately and rapidly started to grow. "Wow, look at that," she said but didn't stop licking. "Is there no more pee coming?" she asked.

"No," I said, "but if you keep doing that then it'll do what it did earlier today."

"What do you mean it'll shoot all that white stuff out? I've gotta see this."

"Well if you really want to see it, put your lips around it and suck while you move it in and out of your mouth". Which she immediately did, gazing up at my face. You would have thought she had been doing it for years, she was a natural. Her mouth swallowed me deep inside and her hands rubbed the shaft.

What I sight, that beautiful young and innocent face with her mouth bobbing up and down on my swollen cock.

"Are you ready for this?" I asked, to which she just nodded and sucked and rubbed harder. I felt my cock well up as the pressure reached the point of no return and then I was shooting my load into her mouth. I felt her gag but she never faltered, just sucked all the harder. At last, I was spent but as my cock started to shrink, she still kept squeezing and sucking.

When she finally stood, she said "I didn't want to lose any of that, it was brilliant! Wait till I tell the others that I had a first"

We just stood cuddling and kissing for a while, until I said: "I think it's time we went home."

"I'll see you tomorrow, it was nice having you all to myself for a while, without the other two. I'm not sure what you've done to me but I feel kind of all grown up and so so happy."

As she walked away, she turned and called back "I love you, Pete."

All I could say was thank you but I thought oops as I turned for home.

To be continued.....

SUDDENLY, TABOO BY

BLACKSTROKER

If you're a fairly good-looking guy with a pleasing personality, good at chatting up ladies and move around a lot, finding yourself in the right places at the right times you will have your instances of sex when least expected; that is expected. But suddenly, out of the blue, without any indication, any buildup, any preparation on your part you have a prime pussy served up to you, and that pussy happens to belong to your beautiful mother; then you are one lucky son of a bitch. I am one lucky son of a bitch!

A relative of my mom sent us an invitation to her wedding. It was expected that me, my mom and my dad would go to the wedding reception. The day before the wedding mom and dad had one of their usual verbal fights. The next evening, one hour before the time when we had agreed to leave for the wedding, dad announced that he would not be going, walked out the door and drove off in his car. I had expected it because I knew that dad couldn't stand mom's family and they felt the same way about him. I had wanted to call it off because of the sudden tension, but my mom begged me to accompany her. Things were so bad between mom and dad that for years they hardly spoke to each other and hardly ever went anywhere together. They spoke only about necessary things like bills, and hardly a week passed without them having at least one unpleasant spat, over what to me were trivial matters over which either one could have relented and let the other have their way. But they were both stubborn and were equally guilty at times of hurting the other. I have no clear idea of any underlying reasons for their inability to get along, except that they were both crotchety beings.

We went to the wedding in mom's car; I didn't have my own, but borrowed either of theirs when needed. Mom looked beautiful and sexy in a knee length, bright green and gold dress of some soft, thin material with an empire waist, plunging neck and back. It hugged her ample butt and hips nicely before flaring out a bit. She wore bright red lipstick. Her shiny black hair fell in waves to her shoulder. I can't remember her ever looking so lovely before. Mom is Indian, five foot eight with a small waist and heavy, round, wide butt unusual for her race. Dad is black. I couldn't help noticing, with a bit of annoyance, the many admiring looks that mom got from the male guests. At forty her body had not yet started to lose its youthful firmness and glow, far from it. She was somewhere between thick and thin with ample firm breasts and nice rounded thighs.

The reception was held in a club rented for the night. Shortly after the speeches and cake cutting, the dancing started, at first with the bright lights, but half an hour later they were replaced by soft mostly red colored lights. For about an hour the music was varying genres of up tempo music geared mostly for the young. But then the DJ announced that he would not be doing his duty if he didn't slow things down a bit and provide a blast from the past so that more mature folks could participate. There followed a long session of soul and soft rock music from the seventies and eighties. A few men came over to our table to ask for a dance only to get smiling refusals from mom. After much teasing and urgings from a female cousin of mom who shared our table, mom, maybe a little bit light headed from a couple of glasses of wine, promised to get up at some time and have a dance or two with me. When the song 'let me roll it', which I knew was a favorite of hers, started, I got up with an outstretched hand which she quickly took and followed me to the small floor not far from our table.

From the moment I took my mother in my arms and she willingly drew close to me I experienced a sexual jolt that I couldn't understand, and red flags sprung up in my mind. Danger was certainly here. The small stage was surprisingly packed with both the young and not so young and there was no space for fancy foot movements; closeness was the order of the moment. Mom's big breasts were generously pressed into my chest. It probably was no big deal to her, but it was to me. That soft touch of female flesh against mine on a dance floor under dim lights and the surrounding sights of other couples grinding into each other was just too much stimulus for a hot blooded twenty year old. One minute into the song and I could feel the distinct stirring of an erection. Our bellies and thighs were just barely touching as we moved slowly to the song, and I could feel mom's body softly glide over the hard bump every now and then. My body was telling me to get closer, but my mind, wary of the fact that this soft, beautiful woman in my arms was actually my mother, made me resist the temptation.

Although my effort to will away the erection was futile I at least managed to not take advantage of the situation; I fought against the feeling of hot pleasure and pulled away every time I felt the unpreventable touch of my hardness against my mom's mid-section. But fortune intervened and made things really uncomfortable for me. The young people dancing around us were far from good at the movements and coordination required for slow dancing on a small dance floor, and kept bumping into either mom or me, sending our bodies crashing into each other's. They refused to heed the song's advice and just 'roll it' instead they were rocking wildly trying to show skill where they had none. Mom laughed at their inexperience and commented playfully in my ears about us being sandwiched.

At the end of the first song I attempted to release mom, but she held me firm as 'wildflower' smoothly blended into the fading 'wings' ballad, whispering into my ear that it took a lot of effort for her to be there on the dance floor and that she had no intention of going off after just one song, especially after not having danced for so long. She even said that she was enjoying it! The bumping continued and mom suggested we forget our little foot movements and just stand in one spot. So there we were, mother and son pressed closely against each other, tighter than would have been the case had there been ample space around, just gently swaying to the music. My right thigh was between my mom's soft fleshy pair; my hard cock stretched out across her groin area. Every now and then as a result of a hard bump from one of the other dancers our bodies would press together so hard that I would feel the hot pressure of her pussy mound. I was sure that she was trying just as hard as I was to deny the existence of my erection. She neither pulled away or pushed against the intrusion, just stood there letting things be what they were, which I think was the best course of action to soften our mutual embarrassment. My angry cock would every so often throb and lurch against the soft heat, no doubt getting a good whiff of the fine pussy pressed against it in waiting. My hand on mom's bare back would occasionally forget the facts, and involuntarily give in to a quick soft rub. Mom displayed absolutely no awareness of anything unusual going on one way or the other.

Wildflower gave way to the long, flowing 'for the love of you' and mom upped the swaying, rolling tempo a notch, forcing me to follow. My hardon was only too pleased. She rested her soft cheeks against mine and her fingers sunk into my back and shoulder as we rolled our hips and swayed gently to the song. My erection by this time was beyond restraint and throbbed and lurched wildly. Quite a few times it led my body on a tentative exploration without my willing consent, taking quick little probes of my mom's crotch; nothing forceful or very obvious, but intentional touching nevertheless. And on two or three occasions I felt as if the thrusts were returned, but couldn't be sure. We danced for about half an hour, maybe seven or eight songs before mom suggested we go back to our table. I was grateful for the dim lights, the closeness of our table to the dance floor, and that all the other occupants of our table were missing, because I was sporting a mighty bulge in my trousers.

Back at the table mom immediately poured a glass of wine and downed it in two quick gulps seconds apart. Her face was flushed after the drink, and she smiled sweetly but with a guilty look when she saw me watching her. I was not a drinker, but to make her feel less guilty I immediately abandoned my malt and poured a glass of wine for myself which I downed quite as quickly as mom. We both laughed, and mom using her hands fanned her face, while remarking how hot it was, as if that was an excuse. We remained mostly silent, looking in the direction of other dancers, only now and then leaning in close to share a funny comment and a little giggle. A little while later we returned to the dance floor as the DJ started a reggae lover's rock session. There was no embracing or closeness now, but because of the packed floor and the up-tempo prancing we couldn't avoid bumping into each other sometimes. At one time when mom was doing a little spin I bumped from behind and found myself, hard cock and all jammed against her soft butt. I apologized indicating that I was bumped, and we laughed it off. On other occasions her hip, thigh or flailing hand would unintentionally brush my permanently hard cock.

We left the party shortly after returning to the table following the reggae session. Mom was like a bubbly school girl enjoying her first unchaperoned party and told me how much she had enjoyed herself. On our way home, mom was strangely silent despite my efforts to start a conversation. I glanced at her a couple of times and was surprised at the serious, slightly troubled look on her face. She turned off the normal route, and I was suddenly pleasantly greeted by cool, heavy sea breeze as we were now driving along the seawall road. She must have sensed me looking at her questioningly, for she suddenly told me that she wanted to talk to me in private before we got home; because there was the chance that dad might be back home already and we wouldn't have the privacy, and she couldn't put it off any longer, because she'd been thinking about it for days. On the seawall road she pulled into a darkened area between street lights where there weren't many other cars. At that time of night the seawall usually abounds with cars bearing lovers.

After killing the engine, mom slid a little closer to me and began her talk. Holding my hands she went into a shocking revelation that she had made up her mind to ask dad for a divorce. She said she just couldn't take the kind of life they were living anymore, constantly fighting, hardly ever talking, and hardly any fun together. I was shocked. I know this might sound horrible, but despite the seriousness of the situation, sitting there in that romantic atmosphere holding the soft kneading fingers of my beautiful mother, I felt my cock stiffen, begging for action. I asked her if there was not another way, if they couldn't talk it over and try to find a way to make things change for the better. She remained silent for a while then she said:

"I don't think it is possible Darren, I don't think it would work" her voice trembled. "I don't know...I...I...oh, I'm so confused" she suddenly broke into tears.

I reached over and drew her closer; placing her weeping head on my shoulder and one hand around her back, resting on her hip. She was weeping loudly and profusely. As she wept against my shoulder and chest I stroked her head softly and gently kneaded her body where my other hand was resting. I whispered consoling words to her, but it didn't seem to help. I began softly kissing her head and then her forehead and cheeks. Despite the gravity of the moment I felt my body aching with quickly developing sexual pressure. I started to lick some of the tears from her cheek, and she raised a hand to wipe the other cheek. When she lowered her hand it came to rest, palm open onto my throbbing cock. She didn't seem to notice this and I guiltily made no effort to shift myself or remove her hand. The pleasure of its weight on my cock was just too sweet for me to want to change it. I continued to knead her side as I lifted her face and licked away more tears. She brought her one hand around my shoulder and pulled her body closer to mine. The effort caused her other hand to press down hard on my cock. I felt her body briefly tighten as she realized what her hand was pressing down on, but she relaxed, and made no attempt to remove it.

I continued kissing and licking all over her face and saw a little satisfied smile light up her face. She raised her mouth and gave me a little peck on the lips. When she removed her lips I returned the peck and she smiled. I let my hand slide from her hip and move to her inner thigh, squeezing it gently. I felt a little pressure on my cock and wasn't sure if it was due to its own throbbing or some movement from mom's hand, but shortly after I felt the identical pressure again, and again, and again in succession and I realized she was gently squeezing my hard cock as if testing it's rigidity. Against my true feelings I tried to draw away, but she pulled me back and raised her lips once more to mine. The lips lingered on mine, and then I felt her probing tongue. I opened my mouth and let it in. We kissed passionately. I let my one hand slide further between the soft thighs and felt her move them apart to give me access. I found her mound and squeezed it as my other hand slipped in the deep v of her dress and found its way around a soft full breast. I massaged it for a while then twirled the hard nipple between my fingers. She gasped and I felt her fumbling with the front of my trousers. With my free hand I managed to loosen my belt and unbutton the waist. I felt her pull the zip down and I used my hand to raise the waistband of my briefs allowing her hand to go in. she grabbed my pulsing cock and uttered a little purring sound.

I felt her suddenly break away from my lips and pull back her body. That scared me briefly. I thought she was bringing an end to our shameful act. But she pushed back some more then lowered her head to my cock. I felt her exhale a hot breath onto it and then she was licking her head. She pulled the uncircumcised skin back exposing the entire swollen head. She ran her tongue around the gorge at the base of the throbbing head then took it into her mouth. She sucked on the head roughly, and then holding it firm between her lips she shook it like a cat shaking a mouse. I felt her fumbling with the seat regulator, and saw her begin to fall back with the seat. She let it go all the way and leaned back, at the same time hiking her dress up around her waist and spreading her waist. Looking steadily at me she pulled her panty aside exposing her bushy mound. I looked at it admiringly and started moving over her.

"Put it on me now baby", I heard her say.

"In a while mom, I want to lick you first" I lowered my head and spread the lips of the bushy vulva and began to lick and tongue her hot, wet hole. She grabbed my head and bucked under my face. After a few minutes on the hole and lips I took the stiffened clit in my mouth and sucked on it while teasing it with my tongue. She screamed softly, bucking wildly against my face.

"Put it on me now baby, now" she pleaded.

I got between her wide spread thighs and felt her eager hand pulling my cock to the prize. She guided it to the entrance and I eased into her, feeling a glow of immense pleasure engulf me as I realized I was indeed fucking my beautiful mother. Before tonight I had never once spared a thought in that direction, but over the past two hours I had toyed with the idea until I had begun to really desire it and now it was happening.

"Not like that baby, I want it hard, I want to be punished. Slam your cock into me, ram it hard, make me feel pain, punish me for this sinful thing I am making you do." She went on like a crazed woman, all the while jerking hard up and against me.

"No mom, don't say that, you're not making me do anything. I want it as much as you. I don't want to punish you. You don't need to be punished. This might not be right, but it is sweet and we both want it" I said, trying to make her feel good.

"No Darren, no, fuck me hard, slam into me, I want to be punished, punish me, do as I say." She shouted.

I slammed my cock into my mom's pleading pussy up to the hilt, grinding against it for a few seconds before breaking into a massive assault against the tight wet cunt, pulling almost all the way out and then slamming into her as hard as I could.

"Oh yes baby yes, fuck me like that, punish this fucking whore mother of yours, beat my pussy until its sore."

"Yes, you whore, I'll fuck you hard, give you what you want, you sinking bitch." I said, not meaning it, but trying to give her what she wanted.

She moaned and groaned under me as I slammed into her mercilessly. Tears were pouring down her face and she was sobbing as I piled into her furiously. I rammed her for about fifteen minutes, amazed at her ability to absorb all that pounding for so long. I felt my orgasm coming and with a loud shriek from my mouth I exploded in my mom's pussy. She grabbed my buttocks and held me locked inside her until I was completely drained of cum, holding on to me even after I was completely spent. I felt my cock begin to go soft in her and started to pull out, but just then I felt her pussy muscles contracting and expanding against my cock, massaging it.

"Don't move", she said "just stay in me baby".

I did as she said, remaining still as she worked her pussy muscles and rolled her body under me coaxing me back into hardness. When I was fully hard she began thrusting and grinding and bucking under me until with a loud while she exploded under me. I felt her fingers sink into my back, the nails cutting my skin. Her legs wrapped around my waist tightly. Still shivering in orgasm under me she cried out:

"Slap me, slap me hard". I did as she asked, slapping her with an open palm against both cheeks.

"Again" she said. I complied.

When we got home dad's car was not in the yard. Mom pulled in the door behind us and bolted it from inside, no doubt to prevent dad from using his key to let himself in. She took my hand and led me up the stairs to my bedroom. She hurriedly began shedding her clothes and urged me to do the same. She sat on the edge of the bed and pulled me towards her. Bending her head she took my partly erect cock into her mouth and began sucking me tenderly, obviously aware that my cock was bruised and sore from vigorously pounding her hairy pussy. She carefully sucked me back into readiness. Standing at the side of the bed she kept one leg on the floor while placing the other one up on the bed. Getting onto her elbows and knee, she arched her back and cocked her huge ass high in the air, while looking back at me and smiling.

"Please me baby, please mommy again, and make me feel good." She whispered, her voice sounding like music to my ears.

I put one foot on the bed between her spread thighs. Holding her ass cheeks in both hands I spread them apart as I moved my cock to the pulsing reddened entrance to her core. I eased into her carefully, feeling some pain as my bruised cock slid all the way in. I stroked her pussy softly until she started wriggling and rolling her ass against me, matching my strokes. We continued like that for about twenty minutes, both bodies dripping sweat until I felt her start to quicken the pace as she let out hissing sounds from her mouth. I quickened to match her and felt my own release coming. She hit the tape of ecstasy a second or two before me and we shivered together until she fell face forward onto the bed, me on top and still inside her. After I was drained I rolled off her and lay on my back breathing hard. Her hand found my softening cock and patted it. I patted her juicy ass.

"I feel good my baby, you made me feel good, whatever happens I want us to remain together." She said softly.

"I won't ever leave you" I reassured her.

Just then the sound of dad's car pulling into the yard reached us. Mom sprung up and grabbed her clothes together.

"Quick, put on some clothes and try to unbolt the door before he finishes putting away the car." She urged me as she headed out my door.

I quickly gathered pajamas and slipped into it, shirt and all. When I passed her bedroom she was coming out of the room wrapped in a robe as she headed for the bathroom. I sped downstairs lightly and pulled back the door and released the chain. Then I picked up the TV remote and plumped down on a sofa. Dad entered the door trying not to appear drunk. He was always careful about that. But I could tell he'd had a few.

"Hi" he said cheerfully "you guys had a good time?"

"Sort of" I said grinning

Dad sat down on a chair and began taking off his shoe.

"Where's Gaitree?" he asked wearily

"I think I heard her going to the bathroom a few minutes ago. And I think she has a terrible headache."

He nodded, got up and went to the kitchen, returning with a beer for him and malt for me. Half an hour later mom entered the room, wrapped in a blue silk robe, smelling sweet and looking very desirable. She came and sat at the other end of the sofa that I was on and turned her attention to the TV.

DEBAUCHERY:

THE

INVITATION BY MARINA TRENCH6

9

~Prologue~

I pulled up to the huge mansion in my car. Valet was waiting with smiles on their faces.

"Hello." The young man said, opening my driver side door.

I grabbed my bag and purse.

"Here is your ticket, enjoy your evening." He said.

"Thank you."

I smiled

He hopped in my Buick Enclave and drove off, leaving me there standing on the gravel. I paused for a moment and looked around. All I heard was the singing sound of the crickets.

I slowly walked to the door. Did I really want to do this? Was I really ready to walk through that door?

I rang the doorbell.

A tall white muscular white man answered the door. He was maybe 6'5, mustache and goatee, shaven head, and broad shoulders. I could see the earpiece in his right ear.

"Password." Was all he said.

"Debauchery." I shakenly said.

He looked at me up and down.

"Color?"

"Red." I said.

He opened the door and moved out the way.

I was in.

My name is Kelly Adkins. I am thirty-two years old. I work as an ER nurse. I have been married for six long years to my husband Courtney. We met in college, at a friend's birthday party. He had this sense of humor that drew me in. He was attractive, driven and persistent. He worked to get me. And now, it seems like he decided he didn't need to work in order to "keep" me. Our marriage has been going downhill in the past two years. I guess it was around the time I had my gall bladder surgery. The recovery was a lot harder than he or I anticipated. It took me almost two months to recover and in that time, I gained weight. I went from a size 14 to a size 24. I hated how I looked and truthfully, I think Courtney hated how I looked. I still had a shape and I still had curves, but.... I was naïve, I ballooned up. I did not look the same way I looked when we got married. It took a toll on our sex life. I didn't even initiate sex anymore, and neither did he. We hadn't sex in over a year. My theory was simple, if my husband isn't having sex with me, he was having sex with someone.

Now, I am bored.

At work, about three weeks ago, a woman came in following an automobile accident. Her name was Naomi. I worked on her case, and she and I had a chance to talk. She is the one who told me about 'Debauchery'. I had never heard of the place, until she told me about it. We made small talk. I told her I was married, she is divorced. She asked me about kids, I told her none. She didn't have any either. Somehow, some way, we had a personal conversation and I told her a little about my marriage. It can be easier talking to a stranger than someone you know. I don't know why, maybe I was just desperate to talk to someone. I told her my husband and I were more roommates than a married couple. We talked about our sex life. I explained to her that it has been a year. I remember her eyes got big. She asked me if I had a sex drive. I laughed and told her I did, but that my husband just doesn't find me attractive. I told her, I had gained weight and ever since then, he doesn't even joke about sex, let alone attempt to have it.

One night, as I checked Naomi's chart, she told me about 'Debauchery'. She gave me little details about it, the only thing she told me was "If you want to let your inner goddess out, this is the place to do it." I laughed and told her "my inner goddess is on life support; she needs more than some club to come out." I shrugged it off, she gave me the card and I tucked it away in my scrubs. I had forgotten all about it. Two days later, she was discharged.

Two weeks later, I was home waiting for my husband to come home when he texted me to say he was running late. He was always running late. I saw the credit card bill; I wasn't stupid I was fully aware that he was seeing someone. I didn't confront him, in fact I kept my mouth shut. I mean, he went to Tiffany & Co, yet neither he nor I have any jewelry from there. I saw purchases from Lane Bryant, but I didn't receive any clothes. I knew what was going on. I just wasn't ready to call it quits yet. I asked him when he would be home, he said it would be late, and told me not to wait up. I laughed to myself as I poured a glass of wine. After my third glass, I remembered the card Naomi gave me. I searched all in my closet, before finding the black card with silver writing.

'Debauchery'

On the back was a number to call. I grabbed my cell phone and dialed the number, on the third ring, a woman answered.

"Hello?"

"Hi…. Uhhh…. I was looking for 'Debauchery'." I said.

"Yes ma'am, who referred you?"

"Naomi… uh…. Naomi Watts."

She cleared her throat.

"Wonderful, what is your name?"

"Kelly Adkins." I answered.

"Ms. Adkins, on the back of your card there should be a four-digit code, can you read that to me?"

I turned the card over.

"4512" I read.

"Excellent." She said,

I put the card into my wallet.

"Your password will be 'Debauchery' and the color code will be 'red', you may want to write that down." She began.

"Okay."

"You will need to bring in your test results, those results must be within 72 hours and signed by a doctor." She said,

"Test results?" I asked.

"Yes ma'am, STD results, you would need to go and get tested." She said matter of fact.

"Oh…. Ok."

"Once you have those results, you would need to bring those in person to our offices." She said,

"Ok" I said.

Two days later, I found myself waiting in a room down in Buckhead.

"Ms. Adkins? Come on back." a tall blonde woman said.

I followed her to a room painted in red. The couch and chairs were black leather; the chandelier was made of crystals. She had boudoir photos hanging on the walls, some naked, some in lingerie. I took a seat on the chair and handed over the manila folder that had my test results in there.

"Can I see your license?" she asked politely.

"Sure." I said digging in my purse.

"Here you are."

"Our next social event is this Saturday." She said filling out a form.

I nodded.

We sat in silence as she wrote the form up.

"Ok, here is the key, which is also your entrance in." she explained.

I took the key.

"Your color is red, which just means you are a first timer. You will see people in white, those are members who have been here before and are used to the place. You can wear red as many times as you want. Red lets everyone else know that.... you're new." She smiled.

I nodded.

"There are no rules for 'Debauchery', the only rule is 'no absolutely means no', that's it."

"So if a man tells me 'no' then...."

"No, a man won't tell you 'no', you would tell him 'no'."

I looked down at my hands and laughed.

"Ok,"

"Trust me, you will have a large array of men to choose from." She said softly.

"This is the non-disclosure agreement. You cannot discuss 'Debauchery' with nonmembers." She said,

I nodded.

"Here you are, and remember, what happens at 'Debauchery' stays at 'Debauchery'."

I took the packet and headed to the door.

"Enjoy yourself Kelly."

Debauchery

I walked into the house, the door closed behind me.

"Hello ma'am, may I take your coat?" a tall black man asked.

My mouth dropped open as I looked at him. Before me he stood, wearing a pair of jeans, no top. His chest and abs were chiseled. I was in awe of his body. He walked up to me, his hands touching his shoulders as he removed my coat, slowly off my body. He then extended his hand, asking for my bag. I handed it over. As he took it, he smiled, showing a set of perfect white teeth.

"Thank you." I breathed.

I smoothed out my Torrid crisscross babydoll dress self-consciously. I walked up the grand staircase to the second floor. In the background I could hear the piano being played softly. I walked down the hall, on a red carpet. The first room I passed, the door was slightly ajar. I pushed the door open and peeked inside.

Inside was a California king bed. Candles were burning. I could hear the moaning before I could make out the couple on the bed. The woman, an older white woman was on her back, on top of her was a younger white male. He was grinding his dick into her. She was moaning, grabbing his ass and squeezing. I was frozen, all I could was watch. He pulled out of her and started eating her pussy. I watched her hike her legs up, squeeze her breasts together and just moan. She rubbed his head, running her hands through his hair, pulling his face into her pussy.

I left and closed the door, making my way down the hall towards the living room that was straight ahead. There were five additional rooms that I passed. The last room on the right, just before the living room, was open. There was no door, it was completely open. I stopped in my tracks as I watched what looked like five couples, all fucking. On the opposite wall was a man fucking a woman from behind, pulling her hair and grinding into her pussy.

"Are you enjoying yourself?" a man asked me.

I jumped.

"Sorry, I didn't mean to scare you." He said.

I looked at him.

He was tall, about 6'2, lean. He was white. He had green eyes, wavy brunette hair.

"Hi, I am Anthony." He said, extending his hand.

"Hi Anthony, I am Kelly." I said, shaking his hand.

"First time I see." He said, looking at me up and down.

I nodded.

"Let me show you around." He said, offering his arm.

We walked into the living room.

"This is the main meeting area…. People come here to kind of meet and greet, sit and just talk." He explained.

The room was filled with people, but not overly crowded. All the men were shirtless. The women all wore either white, black or red. I assumed the black dressed women were pretty much experts in 'Debauchery'. They all sat around, drinking champagne and having conversations amongst themselves.

"Everyone, this is Kelly…. Kelly, this is everyone." Anthony said.

My mouth dropped open, I wasn't expecting the introduction.

"Welcome Kelly!" they all said at once.

I waved shyly as Anthony led me down the hall.

"You can choose a private room, or you can choose an exhibition room. The exhibition rooms do not have doors, they have no privacy whatsoever." He said.

"The private rooms and bathrooms are for member use, of course. Any and everything goes on there." He said.

I nodded.

"Downstairs is the basement level, that is totally for voyeurs." He began.

"Voyeurs? People who want to be watched?"

"Yes." He smiled.

"The entire downstairs is rigged with cameras and the closed circuit TVs all show what is going on down there." He said.

"Oh ok."

"All the rooms have TV, let me show you." He said walking into a bedroom.

"This is the chocolate room; ask you to tell by the color. Each room has a color theme. In the refrigerator, you can find wine, champagne and strawberries. If ever the refrigerator is empty, simply dial "0" and a delivery will be made. As for the TV…." He said picking up the remote and turning the TV on.

"The TVs show the cameras from down in the basement. You see this? That is the indoor hot tub." He said.

I looked at the TV and it was showing a man and woman fucking inside the hot tub. She was bouncing on top of him, water splashing over the sides of the tub.

"Everyone can turn to this channel and watch them… they love to be watched." He said.

I laughed.

"What else is downstairs?"

"I can show you if you would like." He said.

"No, I am not quite ready to be on TV." I said instinctively putting my hair behind my ear.

"I would love to watch you." He said softly.

I blushed a little.

"The basement has three bedrooms, three bathrooms, an indoor hot tub, a pool and a BDSM room."

"BDSM?"

"It has whips, a sex swing, chains, stuff like that." He said.

I nodded.

"What is the top level?"

"Top level has more bedrooms, both private and exhibitionist type, also up there you will find the group showers." He said.

"Wow." I said.

"Group showers are just what they are, everyone is out in the open, anything can go on up there. The whole purpose of 'Debauchery' is to make you feel good and to satisfy your every need as a woman." he explained.

I looked around, before peeking through a window.

"Outside, you will find the pool and cabanas. The cabanas can be closed for privacy or open, depending on your tastes." He said.

"A lot to take in." I sighed.

"Don't take it all in at once. You are new, just go at your own pace." Anthony told me.

"How do you know if a man is interested in being with you?" I asked as I moved out the way for a couple to walk into a bedroom.

"Trust me, they will approach you. You have nothing to worry about." He said.

We walked back to the main living room. Women were sipping on their cocktails. Some were being fed strawberries by various men. One woman was up against the wood panel wall, while a man kissed on her neck and rubbed her pussy through her silk nightgown.

"I feel overdressed." I said, not realizing I said it out loud.

"You can always change, or simply get naked." Anthony said.

I laughed.

"No sir." I said, shaking my head and laughing.

"Here, take a seat, relax. I will have some fruit brought over to you." Anthony said.

"Ok, thank you." I said.

I watched him walk off as a waiter brought over a champagne flute.

"Thank you." I said.

I sipped and looked around the room. I was sitting there, alone, in front of the fireplace. It was a lot to take in, but I allowed myself to just watch. I was in my own world when he came up to me.

"Hello there beautiful." He said.

My eyes started at his feet. He was barefoot, I could see the veins in his feet, which made me think he was an athlete of some sorts. My eyes worked up to his pants, he was wearing beige linen pants and a white tank top. Through the tank top, I could see a six pack of abs. I went higher and saw the tribal tattoo on his arm. His muscles were beautiful. He had no chest hair, his Adam's apple was well defined. His lips were freshly moistened. He had thick black hair, blue eyes. His jawline was well defined. He looked like a replica of Jake Gyllenhaal. I had to clear my throat before I spoke.

"H…. hi…." I stuttered.

"I'm Gabriel." He said.

"I'm Kelly." I said almost out of breath.

"May I sit with you Kelly?"

"Sure."

He sat down, giving me a whiff of his Dolce & Gabbana 'Light Blue' cologne.

"I see this is your first time." He said.

I nodded and sipped my champagne nervously.

This man was gorgeous.

"Yeah it is."

"Did Anthony show you around?" he asked.

"Yea, I got a tour."

"What brings you here?"

I shrugged.

"I don't know why I am here; I guess I just wanted to try something new."

"Well, you came to the right place."

"Are you a member Gabriel?"

"Yeah, I've been a member for about a year now."

I looked at him, trying to steal a glance when he turned his head."

"I saw you when you walked in."

"Oh did you?" I asked.

"Yes, you are beautiful." He said.

The way he said it, sounded sincere. And truthfully, I hadn't been called beautiful in a long time.

"Do you say that to all the new women?" I laughed.

"No, not at all."

I sipped.

"Do you want to watch and get a feel for the place or would you like to experience the place?"

"Let me watch for now. I am a bit overwhelmed with everything." I said.

"Tell me Kelly…. When was the last time you had a man serve you?" He asked.

I looked at him for a moment before answering.

"I haven't." I said with sincerity.

He moved closer to me, cupped my face in his hands and kissed me. His kiss was electrifying. The only man I had kissed in six years was my husband and he never kissed me like that before. His tongue was soft and delicate. I closed my eyes for a moment and allowed myself to enjoy it.

"Oh God." I whispered when he pulled away.

"Come with me." he said, taking my hand.

He led me to a purple color themed room. He closed the door, locking it behind him.

"Don't be nervous, it's just you and me. No one is here, no one can watch." He said.

"Gabriel…. I am new to this…. I am married…."

"Shhh" he said, putting his finger on my lips.

"I don't think I can do this." I said.

He sat on the bed, took my glass and placed it on the nightstand.

"We don't have to do anything you don't want to do Kelly." He said.

"My husband and I haven't had sex in a year…. Maybe longer. I really don't know what I am doing." I said.

"Enjoy yourself, let your inhibitions go."

My heart was pounding. Maybe it was the champagne, but I wasn't sure I could do this. I mean, I knew my husband was out doing his thing, but I wasn't sure I could join that team.

"Sit on the bed." He commanded.

I thought about it for a moment and decided to go for it. I had nothing to lose at this point. I sat down.

Gabriel squatted down and removed my shoes, left one first then the right one. He started giving me a foot massage.

"Feels good?" he asked.

I nodded.

"Yeah." I smiled.

"Tell me what gets you wet Kelly." He whispered.

"I don't know…. I can't remember the last time I got turned on." I told him.

"Then let's discover that." he said looking into my eyes.

Gabriel stood up, standing in front of me. He removed his pants, revealing his boxer briefs. I gasped at the size of the imprint in his pants. He was bigger than Courtney, that was for sure. Without saying a word, I reached out and touched it. I guess I wanted to see if it was real.

"Stand up Kelly." He said.

I stood up as he turned me around, unzipping my dress. My heart was racing.

"Don't worry," he whispered in my ear.

My dress fell to the floor, leaving me in a mismatched bra and underwear ensemble.

"Your body is amazing." He said unclasping my bra.

I laughed.

"I am serious…. You should know that."

"Thank you."

He let my 42DDD bra fall to the floor.

"I love big breasts."

He stood behind me, his arms around me as he massaged my breasts in his hands. I was so used to doing this on my own, that having another pair of hands touching me was a foreign concept.

A moan escaped my mouth.

"Shit." I said as he pinched the nipples.

"You like that?" he asked.

"Yeah." I said.

His hand moved down my stomach, to my panties, before he removed them from my body.

"Oh God." I said, trying to cover myself with my hands.

"No, don't…. let me look at you." He said.

I stood there, completely naked in front of a stranger. Gabriel stepped back and looked at me up and down.

"How do you feel?" he asked.

"Uncomfortable."

He smirked.

"You look beautiful Kelly."

My chest was falling and rising quickly.

Without instructions, I laid on the bed, on my back, staring at the ceiling. Gabriel sat next to me, his hand rubbing my stomach. He bent down and kissed around my belly button. His lips were so soft. His hand massaged my breasts while he kissed my sternum. His hands felt incredible on my nipples.

"Oh God." I whispered.

He worked his way up to my breast, taking the left one in his mouth. I gasped as his mouth covered my nipple. His tongue flicked over it. My back bucked up as he gently bit the nipple before kissing it. He moved his mouth over to the right breasts, repeating the same process. I couldn't help it, I needed to touch something. I gently touched his hair, running my fingers through it. His mouth felt so good. His hand moved down my side, down to my leg. I kept my eyes closed, enjoying the sensation. His hand moved inside of my thighs. I moved my legs apart, unsure of what was coming next. Gabriel continued feeding off my breasts, as his hand touched the outline of my pussy. While I did do a close trim, I wasn't completely shaven. His fingers gently touched the hair, before spreading my pussy lips open. His middle finger rubbed my clit.

"Well, now we know what makes you wet." He said.

I opened my eyes to see him grinning at me. his finger rubbing my clit, setting my juices free. He inserted two fingers inside my pussy, which by now was dripping wet.

"Oh God…. you are so tight." He said.

He rubbed with his thumb, while fingering me with his two fingers. I could feel an orgasm coming over me.

"That's it baby…. let it go." He whispered before putting a breasts back

In his mouth.

Within two minutes, I came.

"Oh my God." I said out of breath.

"You ok?" he asked.

My brain was spinning.

"Yeah, I am ok." I said breathing heavily.

I hadn't had an orgasm in so long. Even when we did have sex, I never had an orgasm with Courtney. This was something my body hadn't experienced in years, literally.

I walked into my house, and collapsed against the front door. It was quiet. Courtney wasn't home as usual. I threw my bags on the bed and turned the shower on. Gabriel's cologne was on my skin. I could still taste him on my lips. I couldn't believe this complete and total stranger had given me an orgasm. What the fuck had I been missing all this time?

'Where are you?' I texted Courtney.

'I am at my homeboy's house, remember?'

He never told me he was going anywhere.

'Are you spending the night?'

'Not sure, we have been drinking, I can come home if you need me to.'

'No, just stay, I will see you when you get back.'

'Are you sure?'

'Yeah, see you later, I am going to bed.'

I was not about to deal with Courtney that night. If he wanted to stay out, I wouldn't even mind. I relished having the bed to myself anyway.

Three days later, I called out from work. Courtney asked if I was ok. I told him I wasn't feeling well. Truth was, I was getting ready for my next visit to Debauchery. I went to Sweet Samba and got Brazilian wax for the first time. It hurt like hell, but I made it through. She even waxed my ass. I left and headed to Lane Bryant. I couldn't think about anything since Saturday. I was ready to go further. I had a twinge of guilt when it came to Courtney. I thought about the fact that now I was a cheater too. I felt guilty until I saw our MasterCard account and saw that he had reservations at the W Downtown for that weekend. The same weekend he was supposed to be at his mother's house to help with her car. Once I saw that, I stopped feeling bad. I pretty much stopped feeling anything. I picked up new lingerie and new body fragrances. I was ready for my next visit, more than ready.

Saturday

"Welcome." The man said, opening the door.

I walked in and handed my coat and bag over.

I walked upstairs to the living room, taking champagne with me. I looked around the grand living room. I saw some women in red, like myself. I had hoped to see Gabriel, but I promised myself that even if he wasn't there, I would still make this a memorable evening. I spotted a tall shaved head black guy up against the wall, by himself. I smiled as we made eye contact. He held his glass up and I did the same. He walked over to me, slowly, deliberately.

"Hello," he said.

"Hi." I smiled.

"I'm Koogi." He said.

"Nice to meet you, I am Kelly." I said, shaking his hand.

"How beautiful are you this evening?"

"I am…. I am good." I said looking around.

"Is this your first time?"

"No, last week was."

He nodded.

"Koogi…. Very unique name." I said.

"My parents are eccentric to say the least." He smiled, flashing a Kodak smile.

"I see."

"What do you do?" he asked.

"I am a nurse, and you?"

"Real Estate Broker." He said, sipping his drink.

"Nice, what are you drinking?"

"Hennessey."

I smiled.

"Were you waiting on someone?" I asked boldly.

"I was waiting on you."

I blushed a little.

"I doubt that."

"Why is that? You don't think you are worth waiting for?"

I looked down.

"Sure." I said.

Koogi walked over to me, close enough for me to smell him.

"Why don't we go somewhere?" He whispered.

I looked up at him, into his hazel eyes.

"Okay."

I sat my glass down and took his waiting hand.

He led me upstairs to a private room. He peeked inside before opening the door all the way. I walked in and stood by the Cherrywood sleigh bed. I watched Koogi lock the door.

"Better?" he asked.

"Better." I smiled.

"So tell me Kelly…. ``What are you in the mood for tonight?" he asked, pulling me closer to him.

"God you smell good." I said.

"You are beautiful."

"Thank you, I am not used to hearing that, Lord knows I don't…."

He kissed me, sliding his tongue into my mouth.

I wrapped my arms around his tall 6'3 frame, bringing his face into mine. I melted as his arms wrapped around my waist. His mouth moved to my neck, sucking and kissing. I closed my eyes and bit my bottom lip at the adrenaline that was raging in my stomach. I wanted more. He took his tank top off and threw it on the ground, never breaking eye contact with me. I stepped back and unzipped my dress, revealing the lingerie I had recently purchased. I was wearing a pink polka dot bra and panty ensemble. Koogi removed his pants and let them drop down, showing his plaid boxers. I reciprocated by removing my bra and tossing it on the floor. Koogi gave me a devilish grin as he removed his boxers. I damn near fell over when I saw his ten-inch dick. I became intimidated by it. I removed my panties. We were both naked. I walked over to him, kissing him, my hands resting on his chest.

I laid on the bed, Koogi bringing his body over mine. He kissed my forehead, kissing a trail down my cheeks, to my neck, to my sternum, before stopping at my breasts. He licked and sucked on my nipples, taking one in his mouth, covering it. I was in heaven. His hands were on the bed, the only thing on me was his mouth. He bit my nipples and began kissing down my stomach.

"Oh shit" I moaned as he pushed my legs open.

Koogi kissed on my inner thigh, down the right and up the left. I spread my legs wider as he lowered himself down on top of me. He started licking my bare pussy before using his fingers to spread my pussy lips, revealing my clit. His tongue started licking my clit, his lips kissing my pussy. I closed my eyes as he covered my clit with his mouth. I flicked his tongue quickly over my clit, making my pussy drip.

"Shit." I said just above a whisper.

Koogi ate my pussy for what felt like hours. Every orgasm I had, I was forced to cover my mouth with the pillows on the bed. He ate my pussy over and over again. He ate it like it was his last meal while on death row. He gripped my legs in his arms, I was unable to run away. I was forced to lie there and take the tongue action he was giving me. I found myself grabbing my breasts, squeezing them together. I held my pussy lips apart, allowing him easier access to my wetness.

"Oh shit baby…. oooooo…… I needed this." I heard myself say.

"You like this?" he asked.

"Yessssss."

I moaned.

He sat up after my third orgasm, leaning over and kissing me. I loved the taste of my pussy on his tongue. It drove me crazy.

"Put it in." I said breathlessly.

"You sure?"

"Yes, I am sure." I said practically begging.

Koogi sat up, grabbed my legs and pulled me down to him. He spread my legs open and slid the tip of his dick in.

"OH MY GOD." I said.

"Don't worry, I got you." He said rubbing my clit with his thumb.

He slid in a little more.

"Goddamn you are tight, baby." He said.

He pushed his dick inside me some more. I was shaking, it hurt so good. I moved my hips as he pushed a little more in. We held still for a moment and then I felt more inches invade my pussy. Finally, I could feel all of his ten inches inside me. Koogi started moving back and forth, gently. I held on to his shoulders. He leaned down and kissed me, pushing his thick, black dick deep inside me.

"God that feels so good." I said in his ear.

He kissed my neck, his hands pinning my arms over my head. I hiked my legs up and opened them. Koogi was moving with a more deliberate motion. He started picking up the pace.

"Oh yes!!!" I said as he began fucking me.

I had never in my life had dick this good. I had never had sex this good. I surrendered to the rushing orgasm that took over my body.

"OHHHHHH FUUCKKK" I yelled as my pussy exploded all around his dick.

He held still, pulling his dick out before laying down next to me.

"Oh my God." I said out of breath.

"You are tight as hell." He said.

"It's been a year."

"A year after what?"

"Since I last had sex." I said.

He rolled over and looked at me.

"A year??"

"Yeah, my husband and I don't have sex anymore." I said waving him off.

"What?"

"I know…. I know…. I don't even remember the last time I had an orgasm before all of this started." I said I was still breathing heavily.

"You mean to tell me you are married and your husband isn't dicking all of this down every night?" he asked.

"Yeah." I said half laughing.

"He is a dumb ass."

I shrugged.

"He doesn't even initiate, neither do I."

"Well I took it slow on you tonight, I can't dick you down just yet."

"I know, but damn that was amazing." I said.

"Your pussy can make a man bust a huge load of cum in there." He said.

I laid there frozen.

"You ok?" he asked.

"Yeah, I am perfect." I smiled.

"No sex in a fucking year?"

"None."

He rolled over back on top of me.

"Well, we will just have to change that." He said.

"Please do." I smiled as he opened my legs.

The next week I couldn't stop thinking about 'Debauchery'. My pussy throbbed just thinking about Koogi and Gabriel and all the things my eyes had been opened to since first going.

"Hey, do you want to go out for dinner tonight?" Courtney asked.

"Sure, what did you have in mind?" I asked while signing off a chart.

"We can do Maggiano's when you get home." He suggested.

I nodded.

"Sure, that's fine."

I got home, changed clothes and waited for Courtney to arrive home. I decided to go against the norm, by wearing a dress. I found a halter top dress from Ashley Stewart.

"Hey, sorry I am late, traffic was bad." He said.

I didn't say anything.

"No problem," I said exiting the website I was on.

"Are you ready to go?" he asked.

"Yeah." I said, grabbing my purse.

"We can take my car; I need gas anyway." I said looking in my wallet.

"Already? Usually you need gas once a week." He said.

"Yeah, remember I had to run errands." I lied.

He nodded.

"That's right, I forgot."

"How was your mom's?" I asked while in the car.

"Fine, she needed her spark plugs to be replaced." He said.

I nodded.

"Why didn't she take it to the shop?"

He shrugged.

"I don't know; she knows I can do it."

"Hmmm, I need to call her." I said pulling out my cell phone.

"She is at church tonight." He said without blinking.

I laughed on the inside.

"How do you know?"

"She told me."

I nodded.

"I will try her tomorrow then, if I remember."

"How was work?" he asked as his cell phone went off.

He glanced at his phone, before declining the call.

"Work is fine; you know it's always busy." I told him as we pulled onto the highway.

"Tell me about it, are you still thinking of going to that conference with your sister?" he asked.

"The one in Dallas?"

"Yeah."

"No." I said, waiting to see his reaction.

"Why not?"

"Money, I don't want to spend the money." I said playing on my phone.

"We have the money for you to go…. You should go."

"No, besides, that weekend you are off, so…. we can do something maybe." I suggested.

He made a sound.

"I may have to do that career thing. I don't know yet."

I shrugged.

"Well, let me know." I smiled.

We got to the restaurant and sat down in a booth.

"I am starving." I said looking at the calendar on my phone, trying to figure out when I would be able to get away.

"Have you gotten the credit card bill?" I asked him.

He was mid-chew and stopped.

"Yeah why?"

"I haven't seen it; you did get it? Did they send it to your email?" I asked.

"Yeah, why, what's up?"

"Nothing, I just wondered. I need to call them. I noticed last month the balance was higher than normal. The full amount came out of the joint account. I want to see the statement."

"Well I used it a little more, had to get some stuff for my mom and for my car." He said.

"Oh ok…. Well I will call them, get them to resend the statement." I told him, looking at him, waiting for him to look at me.

"Naw, there's no need, I will show it to you, it's in my email." He said.

"You have it now?"

"Yeah…."

"Can you show it to me?" I asked, laughing.

"Right now? While I'm eating?"

I shrugged.

"No, it's fine." I said as the waiter came up. I went ahead and ordered a glass of wine.

"When is the career thing you were telling me about?" I asked.

"It may be next week; I have to check."

"So they expect you all to just leave for two days, but you don't know the exact date?"

"It's on my work phone. I think it's Monday and Tuesday, I will be back on Wednesday."

"So, it is three days."

He nodded.

"Ok, well…. Whatever the length of time, just let me know as soon as possible." I told him.

"Of course." He smiled.

We finished dinner and headed home. We sat in silence. It amazed me how easy it was for my husband to lie to my face. His lies didn't even make sense anymore. I was done crying myself to sleep, I was done feeling bad. I had learned that while my husband was out, leaving me home alone…. I would be out as well.

Monday Night

"Hey, did you make it to Savannah?" I asked Courtney.

"Yeah, we just got to the hotel."

"Ok, well…. I had a long day, I am heading to bed." I said.

"What happened?"

"Teenager shot in the chest, we lost him in surgery. His mother…. God bless her heart. She lost it." I said rubbing my temples.

"Man, I am sorry to hear that." He said.

"Yeah, it just took a lot out of me. When will you be home?"

"Wednesday, after work." He said.

"Ok, so I won't see you until Wednesday, is this the only career expo you all have planned?"

"As far as I know."

"Ok."

"What hotel are you at again?" I asked.

"Hold on…."

The line went dead.

'What hotel are you at?' I texted as I got out of my car.

"Here is your ticket ma'am." The valet said.

"Thank you" I smiled while powering my cell phone off and walking inside 'Debauchery'.

I walked straight to the living room. I looked around the room.

"Looking for me?" a male voice asked.

I turned around to see Koogi, standing in a pair of jeans, no shirt.

"As a matter of fact, I am." I said I felt my pussy wake up.

"How beautiful are you?" He asked before kissing me.

A moan escaped my lips.

"I am better now." I smiled.

"I am surprised you are here on a Monday." He said.

I shrugged.

"I needed the release." I said taking a glass of champagne.

"I think I know just the thing." He said.

I followed him upstairs to another room.

"What room is this?" I asked.

"The 'heaven' room." He said pointing at the ceiling.

"Oh wow, they have clouds on the ceiling and skylights" I said looking up.

"Yeah, and the heavenly bed, like the one from the Westin."

"Oh God, I love those beds."

I sat down on the edge of the bed, while Koogi locked the door.

"So you need to be released, huh?"

"I don't know what you or this place is doing to me…." I began.

"You're being awakened." He said.

"Maybe so, I know I can't stop thinking about the shit you did to me."

"Did you enjoy that?" he asked while his hand moved up my thigh.

"Yes."

"Let me relax, Kelly."

He looked in my eyes, I leaned forward and began kissing him. My sexual appetite was becoming insatiable.

"Come in the bathroom with me." he said after pulling away.

He turned the shower on as I got undressed. He turned the steam option on, removing his clothes before we both stepped in.

"Do you mind if your hair gets wet?"

"No, it's fine." I said.

I stood in the shower, letting the water run over my body. Koogi turned on the rainforest shower head.

"Oh wow." I said as the water came running down.

"Don't worry." He said, turning me around.

I closed my eyes and stood under the water while Koogi grabbed something behind him.

I felt his hands on my hair, it surprised me and my eyes opened.

"What are you...." I began asking until I realized he was washing my hair.

His fingers felt like magic on my scalp.

"How is that?"

"That feels good."

I leaned my head back against his chest, as he gave me a head massage. He worked the shampoo in my hair. I had never had a man wash my hair before, and that shit was erotic.

He rinsed my hair and repeated, washing it again.

"God that is amazing." I said.

"Good, I want to make you feel good tonight baby."

After washing my hair, he grabbed the Bath and Body Works Country Apple body wash and lathered up the sponge. I stood as he washed my neck, down to my chest, across my breasts. He washed my arms, under my arms. He washed my stomach. The more he touched me, the wetter my pussy got. Koogi sat on the shower bench, lifted my left leg and washed it. He washed my foot, getting in between my French pedicured toes. He used one of the shower hoses and rinsed me down before taking my right foot and doing the same thing. He rinsed my leg before washing my pussy. He was so delicate, as if he were teasing me. His fingers gently go in between the folds of my pussy lips. He used the hose and rinsed my pussy, before turning around and running the sponge up my ass. He stood up as I ran my hair out. He did one last rinse over my body before turning the shower off.

"Here you are." He said bringing a towel over.

I graciously took the towel and wrapped my body in it.

"How do you feel?"

"Very relaxed."

"Good, that is the point."

"Go and lay on the bed." He said while checking the cabinets.

Koogi came over to the bed, I was still wrapped in a towel. He had in his hand the lotion bottle. He opened my towel and started planting kisses all over my body. I closed my eyes and enjoyed his mouth. He squeezed the Country Apple lotion on my legs, before rubbing it in. His hands felt incredible on my body. He rubbed the lotion on my feet, giving me a foot massage. He brought my foot up to his mouth, kissing my toes before putting each one in his mouth.

"Oh wow." I moaned.

He rubbed lotion on my thighs, on my knees before squeezing some more on my stomach.

"You are one of the most beautiful women I have seen."

I looked at him, sitting up on my elbows.

"I'm not too big?"

"Hell no, I love a plus size woman. Just because your husband doesn't see what he has, doesn't mean other men don't. You are beautiful Kelly." He said looking directly into my eyes.

I laid back down, staring at the cloud ceiling.

He rubbed the lotion on my arms, paying attention to each one individually. He massaged my hands, placing them on his chest. I loved feeling his chest. Each ab was perfectly carved out. His body was so well defined. He finished putting lotion on my body.

"How do you feel?"

"Good." I said softly.

"Good, now just relax"

He got up, put the lotion back in the bathroom, and started lighting candles. I watched his ass as he moved from candle to candle. He turned the lights out.

"Just relax." He said climbing on top of me.

Koogi began kissing down my body. His full lips felt incredible against my skin, which by now was hot. He opened my legs, placing each one on his shoulder. I could've just come off the excitement and anticipation. He began licking my pussy. He wasn't doing it like he had done before, he was doing it slowly, making me feel so good. He licked my pussy, kissing my clit. He French kissed my clit. I moaned softly. He slurped my pussy juices up. I had no idea I could even get so wet that my pussy made noises. I could feel an orgasm coming. Without even trying, my hips started moving with the motion of his tongue. My hands began rubbing my body, down to his head. His crew cut felt so good. I could feel the motion of his bobbing up and down on my clit. I found myself moaning louder. I sat up on my elbows, looking down at this man eating and enjoying my pussy. I had never seen anything like that before. I had never really experienced anything like this before, in my entire life.

"Ohhhh shit, I'm…. I'm about to cum." I said.

Instead of letting up…… Koogi went in even more. I couldn't hold it; I couldn't fight it. I exploded, all over his face.

He sat up and looked at me.

"Oh my God, you are amazing." I said out of breath.

"No baby, you are amazing…… lie back," he said.

I laid back down, staring at the ceiling. Koogi climbed up next to me, lying beside me.

"You ok?"

I nodded my head.

"New experience." I said, my voice a little horse.

"Good, you deserve to feel good." He said rubbing my nipples.

"There's so much I want to experience." I laughed.

"Like what?"

"Everything. My husband and I only really did missionary, no foreplay, unless he rubbed my clit. He doesn't like oral, even though I would like to do it. He never went down."

"Why did you marry him?"

I laughed.

"I loved him."

"Loved? Past tense?"

"I love him, but I am not in love with him."

Koogi nodded.

"I have had more orgasms this month, than in the last two years, if not more."

"A woman should come daily if she chooses to." He said.

"I wish. My husband won't touch me, I thought it was because I gained weight." I confessed.

"Regardless of your size, you are beautiful."

"Thanks."

"What else do you want to experience?"

I laughed.

"I want to cum from every hole."

"We can do that."

"I know you can." I laughed.

We paused for a moment.

"I think about you." I said softly.

"In what way?" he asked.

"I think about your body, your hands, your mouth.… I get wet when I think about you."

"I think about you too."

"Yea right."

"I do.… I see a woman who has not had her sexuality awaken and you trust me enough to awaken it. I think about you all the time. I think about your moans, how you twist and turn when you are cumming."

I covered my face with my hands.

"Don't be shy…..... I want to make you feel good every time I see you, every time I get to be with you."

I smiled.

"When you are with me, I want you to be free." He said tilting my face towards him.

I reached up and kissed him, sliding my tongue into his mouth. His mouth welcomed me.

"I want some more." I whispered, shocked at my own boldness.

Koogi smiled, rolled over on top of me. I opened my legs as he eased his dick in. I felt like I was a virgin with him. I gasped as he pushed in. I wrapped my legs as his waist, my arms around his neck. I buried my head in the side of his neck as he caught a rhythm. We kissed passionately as he slid his dick in and out of my wet pussy. I scratched at his shoulders and back as he began picking up the pace. I threw my head back in ecstasy while he kissed my neck, licking on my earlobe. The wetness of his tongue on earlobe drove me over the edge. I moaned, scratching at him. It felt so good. His hips began pumping harder. I grabbed his ass. It was firm to the touch. I could feel the muscles in his ass contracting as he pumped in me. He leaned down, biting my nipples. I screamed out in pleasure. I don't know what this man was doing to me, but I couldn't stop.

"Harder." I cried.

"You want this dick harder baby?" he asked.

"Yeah."

I never experienced sex talk, but I discovered I liked it.

He pumped harder and faster. I grabbed onto the sheets. My bottom lip started shaking. God, his dick was incredible.

"YE…. YES…. OH FUCK…. YES!" I screamed.

I could see the smile across his face.

"Fuck me baby…. please fuck me." I begged.

"Oh shit…. I'm about to cum." He said.

"Yea…. yes…. Cum baby…. cum in me." I whispered in his ear.

"AHHHHHHHH……. URGHHHHHH!" he grunted as he released a hot load of cum deep inside me.

We collapsed back on the bed, both of us out of breath.

"Oh shit." I said as if I was gasping for air.

"You ok?" Koogi asked, still inside me.

"Yeah."

"You ok?" I asked him.

"I am perfect." He said.

He eased out of me, causing me to moan.

"Sorry." He said smiling.

"Do you have to go?" I asked.

"Hell no, I am getting some water, you want some?"

"Yeah, thank you."

I laid back and stared at the ceiling.

"Here you are." He said, handing me a bottle of water.

I watched as he drank his water down. I slowly sipped mine.

"Yasss…. someone finally let loose." He said rubbing my leg.

"I know; I don't know what came over me."

"You stopped thinking so much."

"Maybe, maybe I just got introduced to something I've never in my life had before."

"Drink up." He said.

I finished my water, throwing the bottle away and getting back in the bed.

"You have work tomorrow?" I asked.

"Yeah, I have a closing at ten." He said.

"Do people spend the night here?" I asked.

"All the time, the busiest nights are the weekend or a holiday."

"What brought you here?" I asked.

"Take a chance, I was hoping you would be here." He said.

I laughed.

"And I wasn't?"

"I would've probably gotten some head and left."

"Oh…. Head?"

"You do know what a head is, right?"

"Yes, oral sex. I am not a prude."

"Have you ever?"

"Yeah, in college, my husband doesn't like it. So I have done it before I met him."

"Is he black?"

"Yes"

"A black man doesn't like head? Wow."

I shrugged.

"I am out of practice, but I know what it is."

"Do you enjoy it?"

"I haven't done it in so long, I don't remember." I confessed.

"Then I need to get you re-acquainted." He said.2

CRAIGSLIST MEMORIES BY JC

Well it has come and gone. A great, free way to chat and meet other married or single individuals looking for a lot of fun. To be honest, I didn't understand why people did this till I started using it. But after years of marriage, and a very boring sex life, I found myself drawn to it. So, in the memory of the "Casual Encounter," I figure I tell some of my best stories.

So, first of all, I am not a stud or in shape. I have a shape, and it's round. But I do have 7 inches, and I love eating pussy. So that's how I always tried to sell myself as it were.

I say, "Married Seeking pussy to lick," or "Oral Lover,' to see if I get a real bite. And of course, there is always the mountain of fakes, posers, and a couple gay guys looking. They are hoping I am desperate, I was never that desperate. I even put some ads out there for couples, and yes, I got a few fun stories there too. But I figure I start with one of my first fun, wild ones.

Pittsburgh seems to be the city of fun, because I did start in another place close by but for some reason the sexy, wild, and just insane fun was in Pittsburgh. For some reason all the frustrated, outgoing, and wild ladies need a lot of attention. And well, after years of the same thing again and again, this married man needs to get wild.

So, this occasion I put an ad for "oral lover," meaning I will orally please a woman and only tend to her needs, so my cock stays in my pants. Well after all the fakes, and a few gay gentlemen sending dick pics, I found a very beautiful, and very frustrated young lady. Young to me since I am in my 30's, but she was in her 20's. She was an ebony goddess, 5'4, short dark hair, dark eyes, and had a few tattoos to handle the soft curves. She was not overweight, in her picture, she did tell me that she was 6 months pregnant. and we talked; why was I cheating on my wife, why was she cheating on her boyfriend, and realized for the same reasons. So, she was very happy to meet me for a late night at my place.

She drove up in her beat-up SUV, and when she walked, well, I was surprised at how pregnant she was.

She smiled at me, "Look I told."

I smiled back, "yes you did, and you still look beautiful," I said as I hugged her.

That was true, her belly was big but she had soft curves, big breasts, and very full lips I could not wait to kiss.

So, she walked inside, I took her coat and hung it up, "so in here or upstairs," she says with a smile on her face.

Very upfront with what she wanted, "I figure the bedroom upstairs, guess you don't want to chat first?" I said with a sly grin.

"Hell no, just eat my pussy out," she said as she grabbed my hand and took me upstairs. I motioned for my bedroom, and she was happy, "oh thank god a king size bed, I love a lot of room."

She turned around and met my lips with hers. I felt a rush over me as I felt how soft, and full her lips were. I love how her tongue played with mine, and how she wrapped her arms around me. I turned her around and kissed her neck as I slowly rolled her sweatpants off, seeing that she was not wearing any underwear.

"Wow, you really are ready for me," I laughed as I kissed her neck.

"I need my pussy licked, so you better be good," she moaned as I lifted her sweat shirt off and pulled off her bra. I turned her around and cupped her breast in my hand, sucking on her nipple as my other hand massaged her sexy, round ass.

She moaned, "OK stop teasing, god I am dripping."

I laughed as I ran my fingers over her pussy, she was not kidding. I tasted my fingers, and they were so sweet. She licks her lips as I run my fingers over her pussy again, and this time I feed them to her. She moans as I move her to the bed. She gets on it, spreads her legs wide, holding them, and just smiles at me. I lean down and roll my tongue over her clit, sucking on her pussy lips.

"Yes, that's it. And lick that asshole too baby. No poking, just licking though," she demanded as I rolled my tongue over her asshole, darting my tongue in and out. "Fuck yeah, just like that," she moaned.

She was very much a talker. Never stopping to let me know how it feels, or what to do, just the way I love it.

Her fingers ran through my hair as I sucked on her clit, tasting her sweet juices.

"Oh, mother fucker you got a fucking awesome tongue, don't stop," she cries out as I flick my tongue over her clit.

I roll my fingers over her pussy, getting them wet and slowly pushing them in.

"Fuck yeah, fuck that pussy," she said as her eyes grew wide looking down at me. My fingers would work, curling up till they felt that magic spot and did the come-hither technique on the g spot.

Her body is shaking now, "Fuck Fuck Fuck, don't stop. Please don't stop," she cries out as her eyes roll back into her head.

With one last moan, a gush of juices explodes out of her pussy. Her body was shaking, a wave hit again and again. I pull out and rub her clit furiously to keep the sensation going.

"Oh fuck," she laughs, "sorry about your bed."

"It's alright, at least it was for the right reasons," I smiled at her as I bent down and licked her pussy clean. She pulled me to her and kissed my lips, our tongues moving against each other as I squeezed her breast.

"God, I needed that, can I have more?' she asked.

I smiled and kissed her again, then rolled her over and put her ass in the air.

"My fave," she said as she smiled and put her head down on the bed. Her ass was that perfect round you love to see on a woman, firm and soft. Perfect for spanking, which I did.

"Yes, that's your ass tonight," she moaned as I smacked it again and again.

I let a drop of saliva hit her asshole as I held her cheeks open, then rubbed it in with my tongue as my fingers began rubbing that clit again.

"Fuck, I guess I found the right ad because you are hitting all the right buttons," she moaned as I darted my tongue in and out her asshole.

Her pussy was dripping at this point, and the more I rolled my fingers over that clit the wetter she got.

"Right there, right there, yes, yes, YES!!" she cried out as her body shook again and another explosion of juices, this time hitting my face as I licked her ass and rubbed her clit. "Mother Fucker, you are too dam good," she cried out as her body shook.

She got up and kneeling on her knees rushed to kiss my lips. We make out, tasting her juices all over my lips and tongue. She looks down and sees that I am supporting a very nice piece of wood.

Her eyes widened, "God I love to feel that in my pussy right now," she hinted at me as she grabbed it, feeling how hard I am.

"It Is your night, I am good with what you are needing to be pleased," I smiled at her as the feel of her hand on my hard cock sent a wave of excitement through me.

"Do you have any condoms?" she asked, pleading with me with her eyes to have some.

"Yes," I replied. She kissed me passionately and bent her self back over just presenting her pussy to me, begging to be fucked.

I smacked her ass and wrapped my cock in that condom. I smacked her again as she bounces that ass up and down.

"That is fucking hot," I exclaimed.

"Fuck me, please," she begged.

I licked her ass, "I love it," I said as I ran my cock over her pussy, "do you want it?" I asked.

"Please fuck me, fuck me now," she begged as she shook her ass. I smacked her clit with my cock, then pushed it deep into that pussy.

"That's it mother fucker, fuck me," she moaned as I grabber her hips and begin to pump my cock inside her. I go fast at first, and then catch myself. I slow down and get to a slower rhythm.

"You almost came didn't you," she laughed.

"Fuck yeah, your pussy is tight, "I moaned as reach underneath and grabbed her tits.

"I know, right," she said as she pushed against my body.

I grabbed both arms, holding her up as we hooked arms together and began to pick up the pace. I was soon hearing the sound of my balls slap against her pussy as she moans louder and louder.

"FUCK ME," I heard her as I let go of one arm and pulled her hair back.

"That's it, fuck this bitch," she cried out as I began to pound her pussy faster and faster.

"YESSS!!!" She screamed as I felt her walls squeeze the life of my cock, forcing me to slow down and let her down.

"Why did you stop, you had me cumming so hard," she groaned as she pulled her up towards me.

"I am so close to cumming myself, and I am not down with that pussy." I said as I laid down on the bed and moved her on top, "now ride this cock baby," I commanded as she slid my cock inside her pussy.

I loved watching her eyes roll back as she slides up and down on my shaft, "Fuck I love bouncing on the hard cock," she said as she leaned over and kissed my lips.

Her hips were very talented, as she moved them to rub her pussy the right way inside and to keep me from popping so fast. She moaned in my ear, kissing me deeply. I lifted her up and sucked on her nipples.

"Oh baby, don't stop, you're going to make me pop again," she cried as her hands rubbed my chest.

I pulled her back down and grabbed her ass, spreading her cheeks as I took over and began to pump into that pussy. Going slow and deep at first, then picking up the speed.

"Cum all over my cock baby," I whispered in her ear.

She moaned louder and louder, "Cum with me, fuck please come with me," she cried out as her body shook more and more.

"YES!" I screamed as I exploded the condom. The feeling of my cock convulsing inside her brought a big smile to her face.

"Damn, I love Craiglists," she said as she laughed, kissing me deeply as I rolled her on her side.

"Fuck," I replied as I catch my breath, feeling her juices drip down my legs.

"I think you got my bed wet again," I laughed as I sat up.

"I am not sorry, that was fucking amazing," she replied.

I go and clean myself up, and come back, laying next to her.

She cuddles into me, "for a moment I thought you were going to kick me out," she sighed.

"Oh, hell no, just don't like to have the condom on afterwards," I smiled as I held her close.

"Well I can tell you the baby liked that, and so did I. So, am I going to see you again?" She asked me to look up.

"Uh, yes, I have the summer free so how about you email me when you want to hook up." I said.

She kissed me, "and next time I'll show you my other skill," as she licked her lips.

Covid Vaccine With An Extra Booster

by EliteSoldier159

From a glance, John Richardson looked like just an ordinary 18 year old High School Student. He was handsome, stood an average 5' 9", had dark brown hair, hazel eyes which females found attractive, and a good, friendly personality which people warmed up to. He got good grades, had a small circle of friends, and went bowling on Fridays with his school's Bowling Club. Just your completely ordinary kid about to take on the world after graduation... or so most people would assume. Something had recently happened to him, and little did he know how much it was going to affect his life...

Recently, John had gone in for a checkup with his doctor. Everything was fine, but his doctor told him that he was overdue for a vaccine. John didn't remember which one it was, but he had consented to it. Before he got injected, the Doctor informed him that there could be some side effects, but nothing too major. The doctor gave him the shot, and sent John on his way. The next day was when John noticed something strange. His alarm woke him up for school, he turned it off and got out of bed. He was walking past the mirror in his bedroom when he froze. John had never been fat, but he carried a little extra in the middle. Somehow, overnight, that fat had been replaced with a set of rock hard abs. He ran his hand over his pecs as well, which were firmer, and more defined. He felt like Tobey Maguire in Spider Man after he got bit by the radioactive spider. He looked at his new defined body, shrugged, and headed to the bathroom.

John turned the water on hot, stripped down to his boxers, and prepared to jump in when he paused. He noticed another change in his body. Before, when he was fully erect, he topped out at around 6", now he was probably close to 10, and he was thicker too. He scratched his head in wonder,

"What the fuck was in that vaccine..." He said to himself. As he stepped into the shower he muttered to himself, "So much for no side effects..." After his shower he got dressed, ate breakfast, and went to school. John noticed a difference at school too. Alot of his fellow female students, even some of the female teachers, seemed to watch him as he walked by. It was something that John wasn't used to. He couldn't know it, but he was giving off pheromones that the females, teacher and student alike, found very attractive and arousing. The girls in his homeroom seemed to be eyeing him up particularly, and seemed to be going out of their way to talk to him. They seemed to be eyeing up his crotch too, and he glanced down and noticed that his new equipment was much more noticeable and gave a nice bulge in his jeans. Needless to say he got through a very strange day, and many females at his school went home that night, and imagined being with him.

The next morning, John arrived at school early. He liked to hang out with one of the school's security guards and a couple of the students that got there early. First, he headed to his homeroom to drop off his backpack, it was usually unlocked. But, he found out that the room was occupied. Alicia, one of his classmates, was already there. She looked at him as he walked in, and flashed him a perfect pearly smile,

"Hey, John! You're here early too huh?"

John smiled back, "Yep, getting an early start today." Alicia was very attractive. She was 5' 6", couldn't have weighed more than 115 lbs., had caramel colored skin, warm brown eyes, 34D breasts, a flat stomach, and a toned well-rounded ass. She was a bit of a flirt with John too, messing with him, and occasionally giving him playful punches. Usually she stayed in her suit, but she got up from her chair and walked up to him. Her dark brown hair was up in a bun, and she was wearing skin-tight jeans, a U-neck shirt which showed more cleavage than the school would like, and a hoodie that was halfway unzipped.

"And how is John Richardson doing today?" She asked in a flirty tone.

John cocked an eyebrow, "Better, that I'm starting off the day by talking to a beautiful woman such as yourself." By now, Alicia's pussy was leaking because she was so aroused, and her nipples were rock hard inside her bra. She giggled and bit her lip seductively. John set his bag down in his chair and faced her, "What's with you today? You're friendlier than usual." He said, not knowing the effect he was having on her. Alicia stepped closer, and ran her hands up his arms, feeling his new muscles, dragging her hands across his chest,

"I don't know, there's just something about you... Something that I am liking very much indeed..." She said in a breathy tone, as her hands circled behind his neck. John wasn't sure what was happening, but decided to go for it. He placed his hands on Alicia's small waist and pulled her to him,

"Would you be so mad if I kissed you right now?" He asked, his face a fraction from hers.

"I'll be pissed off if you don't." She said. Their lips met. Their bodies pressed tighter together, John's new cock grew rock hard in seconds. Alicia widened her stance and seemed to be grinding her pussy against him. Feeling bold, John slid his hand down and squeezed one of her breasts through her bra. Alicia moaned through the kiss, which they soon broke, and she looked at him, a fire of lust burning in her eyes, "I want you to fuck me. Right here, right now." Alicia said, unzipping her hoodie and tossing it aside. Normally, John would never have considered such a thing, but today he abandoned all reason and logic. They kissed again and John helped Alicia remove her clothing. Her shirt went next, and he quickly helped her remove her bra, freeing her perfect breasts. They stood out straight without sagging at all. He ducked his head and took one of her brown nipples in his mouth making Alicia moan. She unbuttoned his shirt, revealing his flat hard stomach. She ran her hands along his long, hard, monster cock and she couldn't wait to have it inside her. He helped her unfasten her jeans and he jerked them down along with her panties. Alicia's pussy was hairless and totally smooth. He got down on his knees and ate her out for the next few minutes. Alicia moaned and squeezed her breasts and pinched her nipples as John ate her out.

Then, Alicia stood and got down on her knees. She quickly undid John's belt and unfastened his jeans. She pulled them down and his huge cock popped up, slapping her in the face. Alicia moaned like a whore as she licked her lips, stuck out her tongue, and began lathering up John's cock. He moaned and ran his fingers through her hair. Then, Alicia opened her mouth and began to deepthroat John. His hips moved on their own, sliding his cock deeper and deeper down Alicia's throat. He was a bit too big for her though and she choked. She pulled her mouth off of him and gasped for breath while coughing. John had enough, he wanted to move on to the main event.

He placed his hands under Alicia's arms and hauled her to her feet. They kissed again as he picked her up and placed her down on the table. She looked dreamily down at his huge cock as he lined it up with her pussy. Alicia placed her hand in her mouth as John nudged her wet opening with his cock head, and then slid into her. Alicia groaned, bit down on her hand, and gripped the edge of the table with her other hand. John felt immense inside her, but surprisingly little pain. She just wanted more of him. John began to thrust into Alicia, making her breasts jiggle with each thrust. The table creaked under the force of his thrusts.

Alicia removed her hand from her mouth, and gripped the table with both of her hands. As John fucked her, her body slid ever so slowly across the table, until her head was hanging off the edge. Her fingers white-knuckled the edge, and her whole body was on fire from the pleasure that was coursing through her. She didn't know what had come over her, but all she knew was that she never wanted this feeling to stop. She wanted John to pound her, and then shoot his cream inside her. The mere thought of it made her pussy clench down, making John grunt. John leaned down and sucked on her breasts and squeezed both of them as his cock continued its assault on Alicia's pussy. As her orgasm approached, her body arched more and more off the table,

"Alicia, baby..." John grunted, "I'm going to cum soon!" Alicia moaned and managed to reply through the force of his thrusts,

"Do it John! Cum inside me! Fill my womb with your cum! Knock me up with your baby!" That was enough for John and his orgasm hit him harder than it ever had. He felt as if every bodily fluid he had was shooting into Alicia, whose mouth was a silent 'o' as her orgasm hit her so hard she couldn't make a sound. They panted, looked into each other's eyes and smiled and kissed softly. With wet, sticky pop, John pulled out of Alicia's pussy, and most of his load flowed out of her onto the table,

"Goddamn that was good." John panted. Alicia managed to sit up beside him, and kissed him softly, while John played with her breasts,

"I've never had anything like that, John. Thank you, and thank you for giving me your baby." She said with a wink.

John cocked an eyebrow, "How do you know I knocked you up already?"

Alicia smiled, "It's my most dangerous day, plus with the load you shot into me I wouldn't be surprised if you gave me twins."

"Holy shit." John said, scratching his head, as the idea of being a father sunk in.

Alicia kissed him, "Don't worry, it's what I wanted." The two of them stood and put on their clothes, Alicia managed it, despite being on shaky legs, "Too bad it's not a Saturday, or else I would tell you to fuck me like that all day long." Alicia said while looking at John's cock as it disappeared inside his jeans.

"Maybe we can have some more fun this weekend?" I said while winking at her.

"Change that maybe to a definitely lover boy." Alicia said, winking back. Before Alicia got fully dressed, John took several shots of her nude body, breasts, pussy, and ass. Alicia promised to send him more sexy pictures later, as she added his number into her phone. Just as they cleaned up, the school light's came fully on, and students began entering the building. As the homeroom students filtered in, John noticed Alicia, and another student named Jada, excitedly talking to each other and constantly stealing glances over at John. Jada looked at John, bit her lip, and looked down at his crotch. John looked at Alicia who just winked at him. As the two girls looked at him, John could only wonder what else was in store for him tomorrow.

BARB'S TERRIBLE

CHOICES BY JUSTINAGUY

Barbara Anderson found herself in a situation that she could never have imagined. She was sitting on a bed in a hotel room wearing a very revealing negligee while she waited for an unknown number of men, who she had never met, to arrive and have sex with her. To make matters even worse, her two teenage daughters, dressed nearly as scantily as she was, were sitting nearby in order to watch. And if that wasn't bad enough, there were two men there with cameras to record it all. The married 35 year old mother of two shook her head in disbelief and thought back on how she had arrived at this low point in life.

When they first got the letter informing them that they had won an all expense 14 day paid vacation to Cancun, they were skeptical even though it was delivered by courier. Barb was worried it was a scam, but her husband Tom pointed out that they were not asking for any personal information and provided only a telephone number for confirmation, not some dodgy internet site. So they called the number and by the time they hung up, both were convinced that the offer was legit.

The girls were ecstatic. They had been isolated at home for the last year because of Covid-19 and had been depressed lately. Barb had been especially worried about her oldest since she had just started showing interest in dating before the lock downs.

What would happen when she returned to school in the Fall? Would she go crazy and try to make up for lost time? Maybe a fun vacation on a sunny beach would help her to blow off some of that pent-up frustration.

The all inclusive resort was even more beautiful than in the pictures that were included in the package. The adjoining hotel rooms were big and clean, just like the rest of the grounds, including the beaches. Her daughters wanted to spend most of their time hanging out around the pool and beach areas working on their tans. Barb had begrudgingly allowed them to wear two piece bikinis, even though she thought they were a bit too revealing for girls their age. Her oldest didn't even have a driver's license yet, although that day was quickly approaching. But she decided that as long as she was with them, she could head off any trouble.

And they kept her busy that first week. Her older daughter, Heather, had clearly taken after her mom. She already had full C-cup breasts, a tight butt, and long legs. This made her a magnet for the boys and turned the heads of all the men as well. Barb wasn't sure how much of this Heather noticed, but she doubted the girl missed all of it. In any event, she kept her mother busy keeping an eye on her.

Her younger sister, Theresa (Terri), was more of a tomboy. Physically she was more like her father, although she still had blonde hair like her mother and older sister. Terri had perky A-cup breasts, and even though her mom assured her they would get bigger before she stopped growing, she was impatient and a little jealous of Heather. The only reason she was wearing a bikini was to show her older sister that she wasn't embarrassed of her little titties and narrow hips.

Terri seemed to be content to hang out with some of the other girls at the resort, which was just fine by Barb as that allowed her to train more of her attention on Heather. For the first week, Tom spent quite a bit of time with them as well. He was not very useful in watching out for his daughters; probably because he was too busy perving on the other women and girls. At first this annoyed the housewife, but then when she realized this was the source of his increased libido every night, she decided it was a reasonable trade-off. She'd always had a higher sex drive than her husband, and the gap between them had only gotten bigger over the last 10 years, so this was a welcome change.

So the first week went by quickly and everybody seemed to relax and enjoy themselves. By the weekend Barb noticed that her husband wasn't joining them during the day, and at night he was just as absent. They had been fucking like rabbits for the entire week, so she figured he was just a little worn out and needed a break and didn't ask what he had been doing with his time. It wasn't until the start of the next week that she found out.

The family was on their way to get breakfast when they were intercepted by hotel security and escorted into an area marked for employees only. Tom was escorted in while Barbara and their daughters were left in a waiting room. After an hour a woman came out of the office that Tom had entered and called for Barb. She gave a concerned look to her daughters who were visibly scared, but the woman assured her that she would wait with them.

Inside the office was spacious and everything in it had the look of being very expensive, including the huge desk which sat in the middle of the room. Behind the desk was a fat, middle aged Mexican man smoking a cigar.

"Sit down, Mrs. Anderson." He said.

"Where's my husband? What's going on?" She demanded.

"I said, Sit Down!" He ordered menacingly.

Barbara sat down in the single chair positioned in front of the desk.

"I'll get right to the point. I am the manager of this resort. I have to inform you that your husband has amassed a rather large gambling debt at my casino over the last few days and I need to collect – immediately." He said.

"What? How?" Barb stammered, stunned and confused.

"It seems he loves to gamble, but is not good at it. In fact, he is what we call a loser." He stated flatly.

Of course he omitted the fact that his people had implied the casino was part of the "all inclusive" package, even though it wasn't. Nor did he mention that many of the games were rigged in order to create this very situation.

But Barbara was having trouble comprehending what was going on. She knew that Tom was not a very good gambler, but he was not addicted to it either. He would never spend money they didn't have on casino games. It just didn't make sense what this man was telling her.

"In case you are thinking of denying it, we have plenty of video and witnesses to prove it." He said, flipping a video monitor around.

On the monitor was a series of videos of Tom placing big bets and losing big at various tables. There was nothing she could say except, "How much?"

"Thirty-three thousand US dollars." He said with a wicked smile.

Barb felt like she had been punched in the stomach. There was no way they could come up with that kind of cash. Their house and cars were all financed and thanks to the pandemic, were currently worth less than what they owed. Tom's 401K had enough in it, but most of it was not vested yet; at best they could get $10K out in cash.

"We'll find a way to pay it, I promise." She gasped.

"Now that's the spirit." He said gleefully. "Let's get started then."

"Get started on what?" Barb asked, confused.

"On getting your debt paid. I have a plan right here that shouldn't take more than a few days; maybe a week." He replied.

"What? No, I can pay you ten thousand after we get home and then I was thinking we could set up a payment schedule of some kind..." She started to explain, but he cut her off.

"Oh, no, no, no. That is unacceptable. Once you leave my fine country, I have no way of ensuring that you will ever pay me.

No, this has to be taken care of before you can be allowed to leave." He said sternly.

"But that would take years, even if we could get similar jobs back home." She sputtered.

"I agree, but there is another way. One you have not thought of because you are not the business genius I am." He explained. "All you and your lovely daughters have to do is to make a few videos for me. I will sell them at special auctions to wealthy connoisseurs to pay off your debt. Of course, I will have to deduct production costs and agent fees, but we will have you back to your vacation in no time."

"Videos? What kind of videos?" She asked suspiciously.

"Very specialized erotica. You wouldn't believe what some people will pay to see a mother and her daughters together." He answered in a matter of fact way.

"PORN? No fucking way!" She stood up and shouted.

"Sit - the - fuck - down, or I'll have one of your husband's fingers cut off while you watch!" He growled back.

Barbara sat back down, fear beginning to grip her mind.

"Don't ever yell at me again, or your husband will pay the price. Do you understand?" He asked.

Unable to talk, she just nodded.

"Now, you may be thinking that you can go to the police, but I wouldn't advise it. The chief of police is my brother in law, so he's not going to take the word of a gringo snob like you over me. He might even throw you and your daughters in prison just for wasting his time, and let me tell you, white women never come out of a Mexican prison the way they went in, if they even come out at all." He warned. "So if you want your family to come out of this in one piece, you will do as I say and not talk back."

Barb was numb, but still managed to nod her head again.

"OK, let's get back to the business at hand. I have two stories ready to go. I think the first one will bring in more money, but I will let you choose which one we make. Isn't that fair?" He said happily, but before she could respond he continued. "Now in this first one the mother, that's you, is stripped and tied down on a Sybian machine. You know what a Sybian is?"

"Yes." Barbara whispered.

"Good, good. Clips are clamped onto her nipples and the machine is started on low. Then her daughters are brought into the room by six strong men. They roughly strip off the girl's clothes and paw aggressively at their soft teenage bodies. Then the men savagely take their virginity with their large cocks – your daughters are virgins, yes?" He asked.

The housewife was too terrified to even compose an answer.

"Well hopefully they are; it will bring a bigger price if they bleed. Anyway, as the men continue to fuck the helpless girls, the intensity of the Sybian machine is turned up and up until the mother is forced to have an orgasm while her daughters are taken again and again, sometimes by more than one man at a time. By the time the video ends, the girls have been well fucked in all their holes at least once by each man and have cum dripping off their bodies everywhere. The mother at this point is exhausted from having so many orgasms and can barely crawl to her daughters to comfort them." He finished.

Barb was in a state of shock, but knew that she would do anything to avoid making that video. Anything.

"My second idea is a bit more tame, but I think it could still sell well. In this video the slut housewife wants to teach her daughters all about sex, so she gets a hotel room and invites some men to gangbang her while the girls watch. They all have large cocks and as they see their mom cum multiple times, they end up getting so excited that they expose themselves and masturbate until they cum. When the men see this, they offer their cocks to the daughters who clean them off and get them hard again so they can fuck the mother more. The video ends with the mother and daughters naked in the bed with the girls cuddling with their well fucked mom." The fat man recited.

As bad as that story sounded to Barbara, it was infinitely more preferable to the first one. While she had never been involved in a gangbang before, she did have a threesome once with a boyfriend and his brother, so she thought this was something she could do to protect her family. It wouldn't be easy to do in front of her daughters and hoped it wouldn't traumatize them too much, but this was the best of all the bad choices open to her.

"Number two. I can do number two." She croaked. "But I'll need to explain this to my daughters or they'll freak out."

"I'll give you a few minutes with them out in the waiting room before we go over to the studio." He replied.

Heather and Terri were, of course, shocked, but actually took it pretty well all things considered.

"I'm so sorry about this girls, you shouldn't have to go through this, but I can't see another way out at the moment." Barb told them with tears in her eyes.

"Don't worry about us Mom." Terri said with more confidence than she felt. "We can handle it."

"Yeah, it's not like we haven't seen porn on the Internet or masturbated before." Heather added.

"But not your mother and not on camera." Barb pointed out.

"True, but I'm more worried about you. Are you sure you can handle a gangbang? I mean, we don't even know how many men there's going to be." Heather said.

"I'm not as innocent as you think. I was a bit of a wild girl before I met your Father. I'll be OK." She responded.

The "studio" turned out to be one of the hotel suites with an adjoining room used as a dressing and makeup room. That's where they met the "director" of the video, a young Mexican woman named Maria. The first thing she said was, "Get out of your clothes so I can see what I have to work with."

Her daughters were a bit shy to strip in front of a stranger, so Barbara went first and quickly pulled off her sundress and shimmied out of her swimsuit. This did seem to give the teens some courage and soon they were all naked. Maria studied them and then pointed to Barb.

"I like the landing strip, but you need to shave the rest." She said.

The mother of two did not have a very thick bush, so she liked to keep it shaved except for a small strip above her labia. But she hadn't shaved all week, and some stubble was showing.

"You two, I want you completely bald." Maria stated while pointing to Heather and her younger sister.

"Bald?" Terri asked, confused.

"No pussy hair. Bald cunt." Maria said bluntly.

It looked to Barb like her older daughter probably trimmed her pubic hair so it didn't stick out her bikini bottoms, but never shaved. Like her mother, her bush was not very thick, so she must have felt it wasn't necessary. Terri only had a light layer of fuzz that hardly showed, but apparently even that was too much hair for Maria.

So Barb took to the shower to show her girls how to shave their mounds properly without cutting themselves. After she was done, Heather took her place and she let Maria apply some simple makeup "for the camera". Then she was given a sheer negligee to wear and told to wait in the other room while Maria took care of her daughters.

It was a little unnerving for the housewife to wait, nearly naked, with the two cameramen who were openly ogling her body. At 35 her D-cup tits didn't have much sag and despite having two children, her stomach was pretty firm thanks to lots of work at the gym. She also still had those killer legs that seemed to go on forever and although her ass was not as tight as it used to be, most women her age would be jealous. So she passed the time by studying the cue cards and her (few) prepared lines.

When her nervous daughters entered the room they were each wearing a camisole that just barely covered their breasts and a pair of bikini briefs. Even though everything was technically covered, she could see their nipples poking into the thin fabric of the camisole and the briefs were so small that you could clearly see their camel toe. Their long blonde hair had also been pulled back into ponytails, making them look even younger than they were.

That brought Barb back to the present and her current crazy situation. But even now as she looked back on all her decisions, she didn't see any way she could have avoided it.

"OK everybody, the boys are on their way over. Get ready." Maria called out.

Barb remembered what the fat Mexican had told her just before she left his office.

"Pay attention to the cue cards and just read your lines as naturally as you can. But the most important thing is to stay in character. You are a cock hungry slut that loves to fuck and can't get enough. You have to convince the audience that you are enjoying every second and don't want it to end. In fact, if you can convince your daughters of that, then your video will be a big hit and will make a lot of money."

She didn't know how well she could do that, but for the sake of her family, but mostly her little girls, she would do her best. Maybe if this video made enough money, she could spare them any more humiliation.

Meanwhile Heather and Terri were thinking about what Maria had said to them after their mother had left to go into the other room. She handed them little pink plastic things shaped kind of like a chili pepper and told the teens to insert it into their cunny. When they asked what it was, she told them it was a remote controlled vibrator, explaining that it would help them with their performance in the video. She also assured them that it wouldn't break their hymen if they were careful. They were afraid of what was coming up, but did as they were told for the sake of their parents.

There was a knock on the door. Maria opened it partially and talked briefly to whoever was on the other side. Then she closed it again and said loudly, "All right, get the cameras rolling. Ladies, remember your instructions."

The lights on the cameras snapped on and they were aimed at Barb, making her a bit nervous. There was an awkward pause and then another knock at the door. When she looked up, she saw the cue card with her lines.

"OK my sweet girls, now mama is going to show you how to please a man, or should I say MEN." She tried to say as wantonly as possible without being a caricature.

Then she got up off the bed and walked to the door. When she opened it, she saw four young men standing in the hallway. It looked like they ranged in age from about 18 to 25, give a year or two, and all were physically fit. Barbara was also pretty sure that they all worked at the resort; at least she recognized two of them for sure and maybe the other two as well. They were all Mexicans except for the youngest who was black.

"Come on in boys." She said in the sultriest voice she could muster as she opened the door wide.

The men followed the nearly naked housewife into the room and then surrounded her as the cameras captured everything.

"Woah, this is one fine gringo mama." One of them said.

One of the groundskeepers maybe, Barb thought.

"Fine enough to take my seed." The black boy responded.

Barb definitely remembered him from the beach. He was one of the "cabana boys" that delivered drinks and cleaned up after the guests.

"I think this bitch is hot for us, guys." Another one said.

"Is that right, are you hot for us bitch?" The last man asked her.

She didn't like the idea that for the rest of her stay at the resort, these men would be looking at her differently, and perhaps even expecting her to open her legs for them whenever they desired, but she knew she had no choice but to go along with it for now.

"Oh yes!" She oozed, running her hands over the arms and chest of the two in front of her. "What woman wouldn't be?"

Now their hands were on her, squeezing, rubbing, probing. She was awash in sensations that were not entirely unpleasant. Soon she felt some tugging at the bottom of the negligee.

"Let's get this off of her." The grounds keeper and the one she thought of as the leader said.

But they didn't even try to take it off properly, they all just pulled from different directions and literally ripped it off her. Now they really began exploring her body in earnest. The cabana boy pressed his mouth against hers and started a deep soul kiss as fingers invaded her ass and pussy from behind and a tongue lashed at one of her nipples.

This was when Maria turned on the teen's vibrators causing them to jump a little, even though they were on the lowest power setting. Heather had used the massaging shower head at home on her clit from time to time to get off, but it was nothing like what she was feeling now. And Terri had only recently found out how to cum by rubbing her clit with her fingers, so she was completely shocked at how good THIS felt. Maria was satisfied with their reactions and decided to just let them simmer for a bit.

The men pushed Barb down onto her knees and she knew what they wanted. First she just rubbed their cocks through their pants, teasing them. But soon they get tired of that.

"Take it out slut." The leader ordered.

She pulled down his shorts and his cock sprang free. It was almost at full staff and at least 7 inches long. She grabbed it with one hand while she pulled down another set of shorts. With a large cock in each hand, Barb took one of them in her mouth. She only got to bob on it for a minute before her head was pulled away and onto the other cock.

Pretty soon Barb had 4 hard cocks in her face and she was doing her best to orally service them all. The men enjoyed vying for the attention of her mouth and hands, never giving her a break. After a few minutes though, the leader said, "I want to taste this gringo mama's cunt."

So they stood her up and pushed her onto her back on the bed. The big Mexican pulled her legs apart and pushed her knees back, fully exposing her bare pussy to everyone. Then he leaned down and gave her a few long licks from asshole to clit, making Barb moan.

"You like that puta? You want some more?" He demanded.

"Yes, yes." She answered.

"Yes what, bitch?"

"Lick my pussy more!" She gasped, knowing she needed more stimulation before the fucking started.

He leaned down again and gave her some more long strokes, followed by some serious suction on her clit. He continued this for a minute or two, then he stopped and stood back up.

"Oh, don't stop. Please don't stop." Barb begged, knowing what was likely coming up next and not sure that she was wet enough yet.

The Mexican got up on the bed with her and rubbed the tip of his cock up and down her slit, teasing the aroused woman.

"Do you want my cock?" He asked.

"Yes!" She moaned, trying to imagine it was her husband and not some stranger.

"Then tell me you want my big cock in your slutty cunt." He ordered.

"Please put your big cock into my slutty cunt!" She repeated, resigned to her fate now. "Fuck me with that big cock."

He pressed forward and she felt the bulbous head open her up, making her gasp; he was bigger than she was used to taking. He continued pressing and stretching her more than she had been stretched since she gave birth to her youngest daughter. Then he backed completely out, spit on the head of his cock, and pushed it back in. This time he kept going until he was balls deep, his cock reaching places Barb's husband never could.

"Is that what you wanted puta?" The man growled.

"Fuck." She exclaimed through gritted teeth, just barely holding back the tears.

The young man must have taken that as a request because he started pounding the mother of two with long powerful strokes, making her big tits bounce each time he rammed his cock home. As the pain in her cunt subsided, Barb tried to relax and get back into character for the video. Telling herself that this was just a job she needed to do, she swallowed her pride, ignored her shame, and started moaning loudly.

"Ah, ah, oh my god your cock feels so good." She said loudly for the camera. "Give it to me."

"You hear that guys? I think she needs more cock."

Two of the other young men got onto the bed with them, one on either side of Barb's head. When she turned her head she saw a hard black cock, so she grabbed it and stuffed it into her mouth. Sensing another one on the opposite side, she reached up with her other hand and started stroking it.

"Oh yeah, this is one cock hungry puta!" Someone proclaimed.

Heather thought her mom was putting on a convincing performance, but she still thought it was mostly an act. Even so, it was still really hot and she found herself becoming aroused. Of course the buzzing vibrator in her snatch was helping that out. Her sister Terri was surprised at her mother's reactions; it looked to her like she was really enjoying herself. It didn't seem like an act. But like her sister, she was also getting turned on by the scene and the vibrator in her puss.

Maria could see that the teens were closely watching their mother get fucked, and from their breathing and hard nipples she could tell they were clearly getting turned on, so she turned up the vibrators to the next setting. The response was almost immediate. Both sisters began unconsciously opening and closing their legs. Shortly after that, Heather started running her fingers up and down the inside of her thighs, "accidentally" brushing her mound with the backs of her hands. Terri, on the other hand, was pretending to smooth out her camisole over and over, but was really playing with her titties.

The young man fucking their mother increased his speed, pounding her harder and faster. Suddenly he pulled out completely, stroked his cock a few times, and shot a huge load onto her body. She was surprised at the amount of it and how far the milky white streams flew – almost to her tits. When he was finished, he wiped the last of the dribbles onto her pubic hair. When he got off the bed, the cabana boy took his place.

This would definitely be a new experience for Barbara; she had never been fucked by a black man, and this one was more of a boy. She had not been fucked by a teenage boy since she was a teenager, and never in her wildest dreams did she think she ever would again. He slapped his hard teen cock against her clit, making her hips jump and twitch.

"You ever have black cock, puta?" He asked.

"Not yet." She answered truthfully.

"They say that after you go black, you never go back. And that goes double for Mexican black cock. So are you ready to become a Mexican black cock slut?" He asked as he placed his dick right at her entrance.

"Oh god yes, fuck me with that big Mexican black cock!" She yelled and then pulled another cock into her mouth.

Cabana boy pushed forward slowly and didn't stop until all of his cock was inside Barbara's cunt. She moaned around the cock in her mouth, and this time it was genuine; he was really filling her up and all of the stimulation was making her hot. When he pulled out completely, she was disappointed. Then he hooked her long legs over his shoulders and thrust back into her. He was even deeper now, deeper than any man had ever been before. He began aggressively fucking her, smashing into her clit with every powerful thrust. His technique was pretty good for a teen and she realized that he was going to force her cum.

It was purely a physical response to all the stimulation, she told herself, since there's no way she could be enjoying what was essentially a rape. Then it happened – her body betrayed her as a powerful orgasm swept over her.

"Oh, oh, ahhhhhhhh!" She groaned around the cock that was in her mouth.

Her body went stiff for a few seconds as the intense waves of pleasure wracked her over and over. Nobody watching could miss the fact that she had come hard on the cabana boy's cock. He paused until she stopped shaking, his cock buried in her clenching twat.

"Now you are a real Mexican black cock slut and you will crave it from now on." He told her.

He slowly pulled all the way out of her and plunged back in very roughly. Her body jerked and little bolts of pleasure shot from her pussy to her nipples, making them ache.

"Tell me what you are now." He demanded as he held his cock motionless inside her.

She knew what he wanted to hear, but she didn't want to say it for fear it might become the truth. He wiggled his hips a little.

"Tell me."

"I'm a Mexican black cock slut." She said, trying to convince herself it was just for the video.

"Are you addicted to this cock now, puta?" He continued.

"Yes, yes! I'm addicted to your huge cock." She conceded. "Please fuck me now – I need it!"

He rewarded her with a couple of hard strokes and then stopped again. Barb whimpered.

"From now on, you will never refuse me or my friends no matter what we want or where you are. You are our gringo bitch. Got that, puta?" He growled.

"I will never refuse you or your friends. I am your bitch." She repeated, not even sure anymore where the line was between acting and reality.

As the black boy pounded the white housewife, Maria turned up the vibrators that were lodged in the teens little virgin cunts. Heather was beyond caring who saw her masturbate, she just needed relief and pushed her hand inside her briefs to rub her tingling clit. She looked to her left and saw that Terri had her top pulled up and was pulling on her nipples. Terri noticed the movement of her sister and turned her head to look at her. Heather had a hand up under her camisole kneading one of her ample tits. Then she noticed that the other hand was inside her panties, rubbing furiously.

She had felt her pussy tingle before, of course, when she had watched some porn with a friend or had really naughty thoughts about someone. And she had rubbed her little nub a few times, which felt good, but always stopped when it started feeling too intense. As a result, she had never experienced an orgasm, although she didn't know that.

But the intensity was already beyond anything she had ever felt before, so when the younger teen saw her older sister continuously rubbing her little button, she decided to copy her. Maybe Heather knew something that she didn't.

The cabana boy made Barb cum again before he finally reached his own limit and added his spunk on the 35 year old mother's body. After he got off the bed, he noticed the teenage girls rubbing their clits and tits as they watched their mother get gang fucked. He was looking forward to getting some of that action!

The remaining two men flipped Barbara over onto her hands and knees so that they could properly spit-roast her. As the one entered her well used snatch from behind, the other one shoved his cock into her mouth and started thrusting in and out, obviously preferring to fuck her face over getting a blow job. Only one other time had a man done this to her. She hated it then and she hated it now. It was uncomfortable and degrading, but she really had no choice but to put up with it.

"Her cunt is nice and juicy, but you two stretched it out too much." The man behind her complained.

"No problem." The leader said as he tossed him a tube of lubricant.

Barbara didn't know what was going on until she felt his lubed up thumb pressing into her asshole. Although she didn't really enjoy anal sex, she did allow her husband to ass fuck her once or twice a year as a special treat. And even then, he took his time and went slow so that it wasn't too painful for her. Somehow she doubted that this man would be as considerate.

And she was right. After opening up and lubing her ass with his thumb for about 30 seconds, he pulled his cock out of her cunt and pressed it against her little brown hole. When the head popped inside, Barb winced from the pain, but couldn't say anything because of the cock in her mouth.

"Fuck that's tight." The man said as he pushed more of his cock into her ass.

Barb tried to relax and allow the invader in, but the pain made that difficult. Her eyes started tearing up, so she closed them. The man stopped with only half his cock inserted into her ass, and backed it out. On the next stroke he got close to getting it all in, but it wasn't until the third try that she was fully impaled.

Heather couldn't believe that her own mother was getting ass fucked right in front of her. It was so much hotter than watching porn on her laptop.

"Uh, uh, uh" the elder daughter groaned as she came, squirming in her chair.

Terri was torn between watching her mother taking a cock in both ends and her sister cumming in the chair next to hers. For her, it was almost sensory overload. The camisole was getting in the way, so she just ripped it off over her head, not caring who could see. She needed a release from the sexual pressure and didn't care about anything else.

Just as Heather was recovering from one of the best orgasms of her life (so far), two things happened at almost the same time. The man fucking her mom's ass groaned and spurted his gooey stuff all over her back, and her sister Terri cried out "Oh god, oh god" and then started shaking and twitching like an epileptic. The look on her face was amazing and Heather wondered if she looked anything like that when she came.

"That was hot." The grounds keeper said to the teens. "Have you ever handled a real cock?"

Heather shook her head no. Terri was still in a post-orgasmic daze.

He stepped in front of her. "Here's your chance. Don't worry, it won't bite."

The teenager tentatively reached out and gingerly wrapped her small hand around his flaccid dick. It was hotter than she expected! She squeezed it gently and it twitched – she wasn't expecting that. Then Heather noticed it was getting firmer and longer.

"That's it, little girl. Use both hands. Get it nice and hard so I can fuck your momma again." He urged.

By this time, Terri had recovered enough to realize what her sister was doing, but she wasn't sure what to think about it. She had never seen a real cock before, never mentioned up close.

"You can play with mine, if you want." The black boy said to her.

Terri looked at his prick. Even though it wasn't hard, it was still pretty big. She was curious, but not sure if she should.

"Go ahead, you'll like it. I promise." He assured her.

The young teen slowly reached out and touched it. It was soft and warm. Intrigued, she wrapped her hand partially around it, but was not able to bring her thumb and fingers together.

"Just do what your sister is doing." The cabana boy encouraged.

She started slowly jacking it up and down first with one hand, and then both as it slowly grew. The teenager was amazed by how fun it was to see and feel this happen. Cocks were a lot more interesting than she had first thought.

The man fucking the mother's face suddenly bellowed and spurted his jizz onto her face and in her hair. She closed her eyes just in time; she knew from experience that cum stings when it gets in your eyes. When he was finished, he pushed his cock back into her mouth and demanded that she suck out the rest. When he finally pulled his softening dick out of her mouth and got off the bed, Barb used the sheet to wipe the cum off her face that was threatening to run into her eyes. Then she turned around and saw something that scared her a little: Heather and Terri were surrounded by the naked men and were jacking two of them off! She sure hoped they had been told that they weren't allowed to fuck her daughters, because that was not part of the deal.

As fascinated as Terri was with the slowly growing black cock in her hands, the guy attached to it was just interested in her perky tits and extended nipples that were pointing right at him. Unable to resist, he reached down and tugged on one of them. The teen just smiled up at him, so he took that as a green light to play with her titties more.

Upon seeing what the black boy was doing next to him, the grounds keeper grabbed two big handfuls of tit flesh as well. Heather looked up at him, then over to her sister and sighed when she realized this was inevitable. Besides, the vibrator was still going in her snatch, keeping her on the edge and her tits were aching for attention.

The leader of the group was now hard again, but before he took another crack at the mother, he wanted to try one more thing with the sexy daughter. He put a hand on the top of her head and pushed it down towards his prick.

"Lick it." He urged. "This is one of the things your momma is trying to teach you. Do it, you will like it."

Heather flicked out her tongue and swiped it across the tip of the big cock now filling her vision. The man moaned. It didn't taste bad, so she tried it again but made a longer path along the underside, like licking a Popsicle.

"Oh, that's great. See how fun that is?" He commented. "Now open your mouth."

The teen looked up at him with uncertainty.

"Don't worry, I'm just going to put the tip in." He reassured her. "This is only your first lesson, OK?"

Heather opened her mouth, but hesitated. Then she felt pressure on the back of her head and allowed him to push her down onto his cock. She really had to stretch her mouth open as far as she could, but managed to get the head in and past her teeth. Then she instinctively closed her lips around it and started exploring it with her tongue.

"Oh fuck, that's it." The man growled. "You are a fucking natural."

Not to be outdone, Terri copied what her older sister was doing. Since the cabana boy's cock was not fully erect yet, she got to feel it swell in her mouth, which was a real thrill to the teen, although she couldn't tell you why.

Barbara felt like the situation with her daughters was spiraling out of control, so she decided to act.

"Hey, I need more cock over here." She announced. "Somebody want to fill up my needy puta cunt with some hard man meat?"

The leader reluctantly removed his cock from Heather's mouth and then leaned over to whisper in her ear. "Where do you want me to fuck your mom now?"

The teenager bit her lip and whispered something so softly that only he could hear it. He looked at her in surprise.

"Well, well, aren't you the pervert?" He replied with a wide grin.

He tapped the black boy on the shoulder and said, "We're up."

Then he got onto the bed and laid on his back, telling Barb, "Mount me, puta."

She straddled the man and then guided his huge cock into her well used twat. He let the housewife bounce up and down for a bit and then stopped her and pulled her down so that she was chest to chest with him. He began kissing her to distract her from noticing that the black boy had gotten onto the bed behind her. And it worked, because she didn't know what was happening until he started pushing his cock against her rosebud.

She stiffened and pulled away from the kiss so that she could object, but the grounds keeper held her tightly and whispered in her ear. "You are going to take both of us now, and you're going to love it, or else."

She didn't know if the "or else" referred to her husband or her daughters, but it didn't matter. She would have to endure it. With the grounds keeper's huge cock in her pussy, the cabana boy's going into her ass felt absolutely massive. When he finally got it all in, Barb felt completely stuffed with cock. It was such an intense feeling – a mixture of pain and pleasure.

They started alternately thrusting in and out of her in a well synchronized manner, as if they had done this before. Barbara was so overwhelmed by all the sensations she was feeling that she was unable to do anything other than grunt, groan, and pant. But she did remember one of them telling her that the double penetration was her eldest daughter's idea! Unfortunately she couldn't think straight at the time, so she just filed it away in her mind.

The other two men didn't waste any time taking their turns getting their cocks into the hands and mouths of the teenagers. Heather was a little disappointed because her view of the bed was partially blocked, but she could still hear what was going on, and it was amazing. She'd never heard her mom make those kinds of noises before, or anybody for that matter. She thought that maybe someday she would try taking two cocks herself.

Terri was of a different mindset. She liked sucking cock because it put her in charge, but she never wanted to be in the place her mother was now – being used like a sex doll by two men that couldn't care less about her and having no say in the matter.

Barbara couldn't believe it, but she knew she was close to cumming again. Her brain was being overloaded and she knew she couldn't stop it, so with the last vestiges of rational thought, she decided to just let go for the sake of the video and ultimately, her family.

"Nggg, uh, fuck, oh god!" She grunted and moaned as her body thrashed and jerked between the two young men. They didn't stop or pause at all, but continued to pound their cocks into her helpless body. From this point on it was just a sexual haze punctuated by orgasms for the housewife.

After riding through a couple of Barb's orgasms, the cabana boy reached his limit and spewed his sticky man cum all over her ass and back. As soon as he staggered back off the bed, he was replaced with the man that Heather had been blowing. He really wanted to sink his manhood into that ass since he hardly ever got the opportunity due to his size.

Barb was dimly aware that something large was being pushed into her ass, larger than before. It was painful at first, but for some reason she didn't really care. Maybe it was because all her nerve endings down there had become so hypersensitive that it was all a mass of pain and extreme pleasure mixed together. And as another orgasm built, all logical thoughts were once again pushed out of her mind.

Maria, hoping to get everybody to cum altogether, turned up the girl's vibrators to their highest setting. Heather was rubbing her clit for all she was worth while her sister was still bobbing up and down on the young Mexican man's cock while fingering her own little button. Everybody was right on the edge.

Then the man in Barbara's pussy grunted and bucked, shooting his baby makers into her womb. This triggered another massive orgasm for the housewife, causing her to moan loudly and clamp down on both the cocks fucking her. The man ramming his cock into her tight ass couldn't hold back anymore and sent a fountain of jism flying up over her ass and onto her back. Heather had never seen anything so hot.

"I'm cummmmmmmming!" She screamed as her eyes rolled back into her head and her entire body jerked again and again.

The last man loved seeing Heather's tits bounce and shake as she came. He pulled his cock out of the younger teen's mouth and pushed her back in her chair. He jacked his cock a few times as he watched her openly masturbating right in front of him. Then he aimed his cock at her tits and let it fly. When Terri felt the hot cum hit her titties, it pushed her over the edge.

"Oh, oh, oh, god!" She moaned. "Uh, uh, oh god."

Her climax went on and on for what seemed like a long time, but was really only 5 or 10 seconds. Maria turned off the vibrators and after the teenagers recovered their senses a bit, the cameras turned to the bed. Maria whispered to the two girls to join their mother on the bed. They laid down on either side of her and put their arms around her in an attempt to comfort the exhausted woman.

The cameras captured this last scene, and then were turned off. Maria thought her boss would be very happy with this video; maybe she would even get a bonus this time. After the men had dressed she shooed them out of the room. Then she informed Barb and her two daughters they had a half an hour to get cleaned up and dressed, unless they wanted to return to their rooms as they were.

Lightning Source UK Ltd.
Milton Keynes UK
UKHW011824090223
416682UK00001B/156